TERROR RIVER

A Novel

Jocelyn Miller

Eagletalon Books
Cambridge, MD 21613
Publisher's Note: This is a work of fiction. Names, characters, places, and incidents are a product of the author's imagination. Locales and public names are sometimes used for atmospheric purposes. Any resemblance to actual people, living or dead, or to businesses, companies, events, institutions, or locales is completely coincidental.

Book Layout © 2014 BookDesignTemplates.com

Book Title/ Author Name. -- 1st ed.
ISBN 0988621436

Special thanks to Captain Kyle Waltemyer of Scuba Quest, Cape Coral, FL

Thanks to my editors Sally Bright and Carolyn Carson

Thanks to Jamie Anders for another wonderful cover

Thanks to my husband, Bernard, for his endless support and ideas

The story of "Snapper" is complete fiction, and not a green light to kill turtles. According to the World Wildlife Federation, the Alligator Snapping Turtle is #6 on the Most Endangered Species list. Please protect these amazing creatures!

Jocelyn Miller

CONTENTS

CHAPTER 1 9

CHAPTER 2 13

CHAPTER 3 19

CHAPTER 4 27

CHAPTER 5 30

CHAPTER 6 37

CHAPTER 7 42

CHAPTER 8 50

CHAPTER 9 56

CHAPTER 10 66

CHAPTER 11 68

CHAPTER 12 75

CHAPTER 13 83

CHAPTER 14 86

CHAPTER 15 90

CHAPTER 16 93

CHAPTER 17 95

CHAPTER 18 101

CHAPTER 19 105

CHAPTER 20 113

CHAPTER 21 118

CHAPTER 22 125

CHAPTER 23 137

CHAPTER 24 144

CHAPTER 25 151

CHAPTER 26 163

CONTENTS continued…

CHAPTER 27..168

CHAPTER 28..173

CHAPTER 29..184

CHAPTER 30..189

CHAPTER 31..195

CHAPTER 32..204

While most of the attributes of the amazing creature in this story are realistic, its size has been grossly exaggerated for the sole purpose of entertainment

Jennifer Harley's laughter echoed throughout the forest of pines that lined the riverbank. It was well after sunset, dark as pitch in the woods aside from a spattering of moonlight, but it didn't scare her one bit. These were her woods, the woods she had grown up with, and she knew she was safe from harm. Every now and then a delighted shriek from her lips bounced off the toughened bark of pines, resonated through the stately forest and was answered with a growl by Jason Jones who ran behind the silly girl pretending to be a bear, or tiger, or some such thing.

Jason had parked his father's car in the small graveled lot that had been cut into the woods many years before by the Department of Natural Resources. The parking lot opened to a narrow, dirt-packed path that led a winding trail to the river bank, which was a favorite spot of teenagers for beer parties, necking and more, swimming, camping, and sometimes just plain old contemplation. Tonight it was to serve for all of the above.

Approaching the end of their teen years, Jennifer and Jason had been sweethearts since the age of fourteen, and it was now official that the future included marriage. But for now they would enjoy the end of their carefree days before solid adulthood and responsibility set in. Tonight, they would celebrate their engagement with a camp-out by the river.

Jason huffed as he chased his girl down the path. His backpack grew heavier with his antics, and he stopped a moment, hands on knees, to catch his breath. Jennifer continued her romp, shrieking delightfully, though ignorant that Jason had stopped the chase. When she broke through woods to the riverbank, she paused a moment and looked behind to the darkened hole from which she had just emerged. No Jason. She set her own backpack—much lighter than Jason's—on the ground.

"You are always late, Jason Jones!" she yelled and then pulled her pink tee-shirt over her head. Next came the sneakers, then the jeans. Moonlight bounced off a rhinestone pierced through her naval. Standing in panties and bra, she stuck a toe into the lapping water of the river and decided the temperature was favorable for a moonlit swim. She would call to him from out there—out there in the beautiful river. *Won't he be surprised!* While the woods didn't scare her a wit, sometimes the river did, and Jason was well aware of how she felt about late night swimming. Yes, she would surprise him by being brave.

To avoid a slow and shivery entry to the river, she ran through the shallow river's edge until the bank dipped deeper and she couldn't lift her feet above the water's surface. Headlong, she dove and stroked further out, knowing full well that there was a stationary float to rest on; she could see it vaguely outlined in the moonlight. She turned to see if Jason had materialized yet on the moonlit river bank; he had not. When she turned again to the float, she was shocked to see that it was gone! She stopped and tread the water, scanning the river. *There it is!* However, it seemed strange that it wasn't in the same place that she had spotted it first. Again she scanned the river, and was surprised to see another float. Perhaps she was disorientated? It was a confusing enough occurrence to cancel her surprise for Jason. She changed direction and headed toward shore where she hoped he would waiting.

"It's about time," she said walking up the bank, dripping wet and cold. "I hope you have a towel in that backpack. I was trying to surprise you, since you know how I get about the river swimming, but the oddest thing happened. First, I saw the float, then it disappeared and then when I looked again, there were *two* floats!"

Jason plopped the large backpack on the ground and knelt to unzip a large pocket. "And of course I have a towel… "*Be prepared— it's the Boy Scouts marching song!*'" He then looked out at the river basking in the glow of the moon. "I only see one float. You're seeing things. Get your eyes checked."

Jennifer whacked him with the towel, then stood beside him scanning the river for herself as she dried her shivering body. "Well, for Pete's sake. I could swear on a stack of Bibles I saw two floats out there. What took you so long, anyway?"

"I had a lot more to carry than you did, Miss Fluff-off. While you were prancing down the lane, I was hefting all the camping supplies, including the tent."

With that said, he found a spot to pitch the pup tent; a tent just big enough for two. "Okay, woman, get into camping mode and get busy." She busied herself changing to pajamas, which were nothing more than another tee and flannel drawstring pants and then helped Jason set the camp.

When finished, Jason looked again at the moonlit ripples of the river. "You're right, I see two floats now. Look over there," he pointed upriver. "Looks like the float has multiplied. Maybe another float was necessary for the big crowds?" he said, sarcastically, stretching his arms to indicate an invisible crowd.

Jennifer was mystified; she had aimed her swim directly for the float and it, at that time, was not where it was now; she was sure of it. "I don't get it," she said, and then let it slip from her mind as they busied themselves with campfire cooking.

When at last they snuggled into the tent, it was well after midnight and growing chilly. They made love and lay in each other's arms in one sleeping bag listening to the night sounds before dozing off to sleep.

* * *

Something woke her. A smell? A sound? She wasn't quite sure, as she had been dreaming. "Drat," she mumbled, and snuggled closer to Jason. She hated being wakened from a good dream, and she was sure it was good one at that. But there it was again, whatever had woken her; a smell *and* a sound. She rose onto her elbows. Something was shuffling about the campsite and it smelled to high heaven. Unzipping herself from the sleeping bag, she crept on all fours to the tent flap and peeked out. It was oddly dark outside. She blinked away the sleep and looked again. Something big was in front of her, blocking her vision of the river, and it was *moving!* Goosebumps prickled her flesh as she backed up silently until she was near Jason's ear. "Shhh," she whispered, her voice shaky. "Jason, wake up. There's something out there, and it's huge!"

"What?" he asked sleepily.

She covered his mouth with her hand. "Shhh." She could barely control her rising terror. She hadn't recognized what it was, but it was very large and she instinctively knew it presented a danger.

Jason removed her hand from his mouth. "What in the world are you doing?"

"Shut-up! There's something out there. I don't know what it is!" Her heart pounded in her ears.

"Give me the flashlight," he said.

"No! It'll know we're in here!"

"Give me the damn light!" His voice had risen now, which created only heavier shuffling from the thing outside the tent. "Whatever it is, it stinks." He felt for the flashlight, which had settled between him and the slopping tent wall. "Got it," he said and turned it on.

"Turn it off!" Jennifer reached for the light, but he swung it high over his head. "Cut it out!" he said, now crawling toward the flap. "I have to see what's out there."

As he opened the flap, a tremendous blur burst through the tent, knocking it off its pegs and tumbling it backward, leaving its occupants exposed to the night and the horror that now presented itself in deadly force. Jason yelled as the flashlight flew from his hand. Knocked onto his back, he pounded violently on a hard surface that now rose a few feet over his prone torso. As he attempted to scooch from under the beast, a sharp and searing pain shot through his abdomen. He couldn't move; he could barely breathe.

"Run!" he yelled hoarsely to Jennifer— but she couldn't run. Her screams trilled through the night as the creature pierced her between his mighty jaws, lifting her high above the ground. Her sudden silence was all Jason heard before the sharp object that had impaled him, ripped his belly open.

In the woods that could bring no harm, the young lovers vanished.

CHAPTER TWO

August 2015

Theodor (Ted for short) Henry Lane stood on the riverbank, a hand shadowing his eyes against the bright midday sun. "What *is* that?" This he said to no one, as he was alone alongside the river. It was a wide river that quivered and rolled its way toward the Atlantic, just as it had for thousands of years. Pine and deciduous trees lined its banks, and the mighty live oak, its branches laden with Spanish moss, gently swept the sparkling countless ripples that passed beneath its outstretched boughs. It was not a tidal river, but one that flowed by the rule of rain; much rain meant high water that moved swiftly through its course; no rain presented a body of water that evaporated inch by inch in the hot sun and appeared to stand still.

In the dry times, a telltale water line from the previous high waters was obvious on the damp and darkened roots of trees that stood abruptly exposed to the river's will. The bank appeared as if the earth had been sliced in half like a cake, allowing a peek at the contents hidden within. At those times, it was a mystery why the trees did not keel over and wash away down the river. Some did, of course, piling up and creating dams that needed to be dislodged by the machines and hands of man.

But the rains of late had been heavy, allowing the river to flow gracefully to the sea, setting a new high water line by which to measure the next dry spell. Here, on a hot Georgia day, Ted spotted the strange and seemingly stationary object protruding above the water line. A few curiously irregular mottled peaks poked through the river's surface drawing him closer to the water's edge. Here, the riverbank was sloped and led gently to the water. Local folks used this entrance as a small boat launch. He removed his shoes and socks to step into the water where the grainy slope of the ramp tickled his tender and bare feet. Still, he could not get a good look at the strange protrusion. He turned and walked up the bank to the fallen tree that had washed up to this spot many years ago after a forgotten spring storm; he would swim to the strange object.

Off came the clothes, neatly folded and stacked atop the log. He figured he had better leave the jockey shorts on just in case someone showed up to put their boat in the water. He was a tidy person, and set his shoes together on the ground beside the log and his neat stack of clothing. Perhaps he would have time to let the jockey shorts dry before redressing.

Yes, the water was good, cool and refreshing. He found the current gentle, allowing him to stroke his way toward the river's center. Halfway to the object, he stopped and stretched his six foot frame to measure the depth with his toes—almost, but not quite. If he slipped his head below the surface and shot downward like an arrow, he could feel smooth rocks and muck with his toes, therefore judging the lodged object as taller than he; its width, he could not determine. He squinted as he tread, but still could not make out the green-brown peaked lumps. He had never seen anything like it in the river; it did not register in his memory, and it made no sense. It was not a car, or any kind of vehicle. It was not a tree dislodged from upstream, a boulder, or any object he recognized. Now, as he continued his approach, the strange object seemed to shift a bit—or was it a trick created by the gently moving current and blazing sun? When air bubbles boiled on the river's surface, his hackles rose. Then, the mysterious object shifted again—a slight shift—enough for him to consider swimming back to shore and returning with his skiff to investigate safely from on board. *Chicken,* he called himself; and ignoring the internal warning signal, he swam a bit closer. When the tallest mottled peak of the object was five or six feet away, his left toe struck something— something rough, sharp, *and moving.*

A howl ricocheted down the moss draped lazy river in alarming clarity as Ted realized that whatever the strange object was that he had been searching for, had attacked! Birds squawked at the frightening interruption to their feeding, and wings flapped as they took flight for safer ground. The peaked object that had sat dormant in the middle of the river had come to life! *It* pulled him under with little, if any, exertion and he was at the beast's mercy.

Ted had ignored the warning—the red flags—and now he grasped at river grass, bounced over rocks and clawed at the muddy bottom of the river fiercely trying to free himself from the painful grip on his left leg. His lungs were bursting—screaming for air—but no matter how hard he fought, he couldn't release himself from whatever had pulled him under; it was much stronger than he.

The creature then turned, changing direction, and now Ted faced a rock hard surface. He was beneath the creature with the river flowing between him and the murky bottom. His leg twisted unnaturally, sending searing pain to his hip, and then he was free! He tried to swim, not knowing in which direction to head, but could not propel himself quickly away. He was free from the beast, and yet he felt weakened, unable to move. Warm water gushed around his injured leg, but he ignored the impulse to stop a moment and examine his injury. *Swim! Hurry!* His arms flopped impotently on the river's surface, but inch by inch he moved forward, toward the shore— whichever shore it was, he did not know— but it appeared to be miles and miles away. His eyes blurred; he was strangely exhausted. Then, with the force of a semi-truck, the beast struck again, piercing him between its mighty jaws.

Now submerged, his arms flailed against the horrific head of what held him, but that was the least of his problems; *he needed air.* Then, *a horrible mistake.* An instinctive gasp for air filled his lungs with river water and soon his eyes dimmed, the pain in his leg ceased and a peace overcame him as he drifted into darkness.

* * *

"I'll be danged if I know what happened to him. Maybe drunk and sleeping it off?" Captain John Gustard, 'Gus', for short, scratched his head, rubbed his unshaven chin, and then flapped his arms like a bird in the sweltering Georgia heat. Beneath his armpits giant blobs of sweat seeped to the back and front of his well-worn tee shirt, nearly reaching the faded blue letters that spelled *Captain Gus Fishing Charters* across the front of the shirt.

Patricia Tripp, Pattie for short, stood back as Gus's offensive odor funneled up her nostrils.

"Sorry, Patti," he said, turning red beneath his shaggy beard. "Dang heat."

The two onlookers stood and stared at the neat stack of clothing on the log, and beside it, the empty loafers resting on the ground. They systematically looked up and down the river as if Ted should show at any moment, but he did not.

"I don't think he's sleeping one off, Gus. He barely drinks in the first place."

"Cold feet maybe?" Gus smiled wickedly.

"Not funny!"

"Just pullin' your leg. That man loves you to pieces."

"Where would he be sleeping it off at anyway? Something isn't right. I just know it."

"Well hell, he knows how to swim. I was standin' right here the day his pappy threw him in!"

"I know. I know," she said, crossing her arms over her chest, and tapping a slender sandaled foot on the damp earth. "Something is wrong," she said, trying not to think of the recent and mysterious disappearance of a young couple last June who had camped out 60 miles south of where she stood now.

At that moment the bow deck of a skiff emerged from behind the thick vegetation that grew alongside the river.

"Well looky who's here," Gus said, and spat a wad of spit to his side. "Ol' cranky-pants himself. Hey!" he yelled to the sole person in the skiff. "Hey, Buzz!"

Buzz Abbot glanced in their direction and cut the motor. He was close enough that Patti saw him roll his eyes over her body. He then nodded his head in a greeting which she returned with a quick nod of her own.

"You seen Ted Lane anywheres?" Gus yelled.

"Ain't," Buzz replied. He was a man of few words, a loner who lived a solitary life deep in the pine forest that ran alongside the river. Patti had never had a conversation with him that consisted of more than a couple of grunts on his part, but whenever they came across one another in town—which blessedly wasn't often—he stared, nodded his greeting and moved on. Even from the riverbank, she could feel the chilling icy blue of his eyes—eyes set close together beneath furrowed brows and a salt and pepper buzz cut.

"Pile o' help he is," Gus mumbled under his breath "Well if you happen to come across him, tell him Patti is looking for him!" he shouted. Buzz nodded, started the motor and puttered away.

"Gives me the creeps, the way he stares."

"You ever been out to his place?" Gus asked

"Of course not! Why in the world…"

"Just wondered. Don't go. That's my advice."

"I don't think we *ever* have to be concerned about that event."

Gus was an old-timer. He and Buzz grew up in the same era, the old days before the onslaught of real estate developers hungry for new land to plunder. Housing developments were popping up overnight, or so it seemed, encroaching on the lazy small-town lifestyle of the folks in Riverside. Like Buzz, Gus lived in a cabin in the woods, but Gus enjoyed the company of other folks. He was often in town having a coffee at the diner, or a drink at the Riverside Pub and catching up with the latest gossip. Everyone knew and liked Gus.

Buzz did not enjoy the same camaraderie. After his mother disappeared, Buzz and his father sectioned themselves off on their grandfathered land and lived in seclusion for several decades. Rumor had it that Buzz's father had murdered his wife, Jane, back in the 60's. When she didn't show up for her checker job at the local grocery store, the job came looking for her, only to find Elmer and Buzz at the homestead. Elmer's explanation was that Jane had gone to Florida to attend a sick relative and had not yet returned. "She must'a forgot to let you know," Elmer told the manager of the grocery store. Jane never returned.

Patti didn't know a soul from the old days, who had ever been to Buzz's cabin, except Gus; she didn't know anyone else who would dare. The fabricated murder story remained local lore and cast a suspicious eye on Elmer and Buzz Abbot.

When she and Ted were teens, it was sport amongst their friends to dare each other to creep up to the Abbot cabin at night, peek in a window and report back to 'the gang' any observations. Nobody ever made it to the cabin. The woods were thick with shrub and brambles and full of enough sounds and shapes to scare even the bravest soul. In young minds, it was possible that the ghost of Jane Abbot haunted the woods and, therefore, Elmer and Buzz were morphed into local folklore, a scary story around a campfire—the ghost of Jane, and the father and son who lived alone in the backwoods of Georgia.

Patti looked again upriver and down. "If Ted isn't back in a couple hours, I'm calling the sheriff. Where can he go without his clothes?"

Beats me. When d'you say you seen him last?"

"Very early this morning." She blushed when Gus raised his eyebrows.

"Get those thoughts out of your head," she scolded. "This is the 21st century. Actually, he stopped by this morning to have coffee. Said he was going to the river for water testing, and this spot is where he usually comes. He said that when he came back we'd go to Lu's for lunch. He didn't come back, so I came here. Then you showed up and I'm glad you did."

"Ain't like Ted to not show," Gus said, lifting his cap to rub his head. "Sorry I can't help you no more, but if he don't come back by nightfall, tell the sheriff I'm ready to join the search posse."

"Thanks, Gus." she watched him push offshore in his skiff, the *River Rat,* and then sat on the tree log resting a hand on the neatly folded pile of clothing. The uneasy feeling in her gut did not leave but grew heavier as the sun crossed the sky. When Ted had not returned by late afternoon, she decided it was time to get help.

CHAPTER THREE

S heriff Monroe positioned his headlights to shine on the riverbank. The night was moonless and black as pitch. Patti had not moved the stack of clothing, or the shoes, and they were just as Ted had left them for his return. By dark of night, the scene was ominous. In the headlights the shadow of clothing loomed like a sawed off mountain on the dirt behind the log.

"You two didn't have any arguments, did you?" asked the sheriff.

"Of course not! And if we did, do you honestly believe Ted would pull a stunt like this over something as silly as an argument?"

"No, I guess not." He aimed his flashlight out into the river for the umpteenth time, but it was calm and told no tales.

The Sheriff's deputy, David Lee, returned from a quick look-about in the surrounding brush for any clues as to Ted's disappearance, but returned without news. "Nothing out of the ordinary that I can see," he said, shutting off his flashlight. "We need to look in daylight."

"In the meantime, Patti, if you don't hear from him by dawn, come on down to the station and fill out a missing person's report. There's nothing we can do in the dark here.

* * *

Later that night Patti sat at the kitchen table, her fingers wrapped around a cup of tea. She knew that nightfall raised the anxiety level, and she was anxious, alright. *Where is he?* She felt downright guilty having left him there—but where? Of course she hadn't *left* him anywhere, he had left *her;* but it seemed that just by leaving the river, she had deserted him. Perhaps Deputy Dave didn't search the wood thoroughly? Maybe Ted was laying helpless... hurt...dying. *No! Stop it!* She mustn't think that way. She loved Ted. She needed him. He couldn't be dead.

They were high school sweethearts. Separate colleges sent them in separate directions, and they lost touch; but once back together in the same town 10 years later, the old spark flamed between them, and practically on the first surprise encounter in the grocery store. More surprising to each was the fact that the other had never married.

"It was meant to be." This was Ted's summation of the rekindled spark between them. Just thinking of it brought tears to her eyes. *Where is he? Surely it doesn't end this way!*

She was alone in the house. Her mother had passed away recently, bringing her from her job as a marine biologist in a facility in Charleston harbor, here to Riverside. Her thought was to settle up her mother's affairs and sell the house, which, having no siblings, was left to her alone. That *was* her plan until she ran into Ted in the grocery store six months ago. Then, selling the house became questionable. She gave notice at work and moved back to her hometown. Love ruled.

She and Ted had both loved the water and aquatic life growing up. They went from catching frogs and tadpoles in the river as children, to necking at the very spot from which Ted disappeared. They grew apart in that summer after high school graduation. It was a time to experience new people and places; it was a growing time.

After college, Ted returned to Riverside to work for the town as an environmental specialist, which was much needed considering the town's rate of development. And here she was, back in Riverside without a job, a wedding in three short weeks, and the groom had vanished.

* * *

When Ted did not return by dawn, the search turned serious; he was definitely missing. A dive team was organized from a neighboring city.

"I have many hours of diving under my belt," Patti said, trying to convince the dive captain, Matt, to let her search with the team. "I brought my equipment...."

"So I've heard, Ma'am, but in our experience, it's not good for a family member or loved one to search for the missing person." Matt, was polite but adamant. He stood at least half a foot taller than she, and it was easy to picture him in his line of work. His shoulders were broad beneath his blue tee shirt, and his arms thick and muscular. A dark crew-cut edged his tanned face, and from it, two intense hazel eyes penetrated hers, as if to reaffirm the 'no' in reply to her question of diving with the team.

Drat. She was very disappointed yet relieved at the same time. What if she came across Ted dead in the river? *Stop it, he isn't dead. He can't possibly be dead!* Her anxiety level was definitely at peak, but having no other avenue of clues to follow as to his whereabouts, aside from the folded clothes by the riverside, the sheriff determined that drowning had to be ruled out before a search could continue on land.

The dive team split into small groups of three. The first diver of each group was the 'team leader and search' diver. The second diver was the 'search' diver; the third diver stood by for safety reasons should the need arise. In this grouping order, a leader and searcher were sent from home base—the ground upon which they stood—across the river to the other side. Four divers searched the deeper water closer to home base, one pair traveling upriver and the other down. The same plan was set for across the river, with two divers headed upstream and two down. Depending on depth, the divers could remain underwater for up to an hour.

Patti sat on the log, elbows on knees, chin resting on hands, short brown hair tousled by a slight breeze. It was hotter than blazes but she could not leave the scene. The sun beat relentlessly upon her as she watched the blinding sparks of sunlight bounce off the river's quiet swells and ripples as it flowed its course to the Atlantic. Other than that, nothing appeared on the surface that was of major concern.

"I won't believe he's dead," she said to Sheriff Monroe, who stood nearby next to Matt. Also nearby was an assortment of scuba gear piled in front of the white van in which the divers had arrived. There was much clutter aground considering the space was no more than the width of a small boat ramp. The deputy, Dave Lee, and the four safety divers stood on the bank intently watching the river for signs of recovery.

"I hope to hell he isn't dead, Patti, but we have to search the river before we move on."

"I know you do, but it doesn't make sense. What was he doing? He was supposed to be taking water samples. It's so darn hot, so maybe he went for a swim, but he was a strong swimmer. I can't believe he drowned. If he's in this…this river, something went wrong." She wiped the tears from her eyes and reached into a shirt pocket for a tissue. Everything brought tears, and especially the wedding dress, which hung within a garment bag in her closet— the wedding dress that may never be worn.

* * *

As the hour ran out for the divers, they slowly returned. First to arrive were the two men who searched the shoreline downriver on the home base side. The two dive teams that swam across the river returned next. None had found anything out of the ordinary.

At ten minutes past the limited hour of submergence, the two divers who had searched upriver from the home base side had not yet returned. The dive captain, Matt, obviously growing concerned, paced the ground checking his watch every few seconds. He scanned the shoreline while the search divers removed their gear.

"This isn't a good sign." Patti said rising up off the log and joining the men at the waterfront.

Matt grunted a reply and then turned to the safety divers who had stood onshore while the others searched. "Two of you guys get your gear and head upriver."

Once suited, the men entered the lake, a fin hooked through each arm. Once eased up to their waists, they slipped their feet into the fins and were about to submerge when Patti stopped them.

"Look!" she said, pointing to a lone diver who had popped up out of the water in the direction they were to search. Everyone breathed a sigh of relief until the man began to yell and gesture. The safety divers immediately submerged, heading for the team member.

Patti's heart thumped wildly. *Did they find Ted?* It was all she could do to control her nerves. After all, she didn't care what the evidence pointed to, he could *never* have drowned and he *couldn't be dead.* She had to believe he was alive; *somewhere,* he was alive. *He has to be!*

After a brief conference offshore, the two volunteer safety divers submerged and the lone diver headed toward home base. The tension fell as thick as the hot, humid air. Patti, Matt, and Sheriff Monroe stood on the river bank, eyes glued on the returning diver. It seemed hours passed as they broiled under the brutal Georgia sun, but the diver finally reached the shore and stood dripping wet, catching his breath.

"Where's your dive buddy?" Matt asked.

"I don't know," the diver replied as he began to remove his equipment. "I couldn't see clearly, but he vanished; and I mean that *literally.* One moment he was there, and the next he was *gone.* Visibility was not clear, sir. We were no more than ten feet apart. I looked over to check on him, looked straight ahead, looked at him again, and he was gone! I searched for him in all directions, but oxygen was getting low. All I can tell you is that the mud on the bottom was churned up quite a bit, and that made visibility worse. "

"Get changed and take a break," Matt ordered, and the diver's fins flip-flopped as he made his way to the back of the van.

* * *

"Oh, my God!" Patti staggered backward, fighting a wave of nausea that promised to surface. She wanted to run from the horrible object the two search divers delivered upon their return. A leg—a leg from above the knee to the finned foot—lay upon the ground. Muscle and flesh, oddly torn, sprouted in jagged strips from its ragged casing. There was no blood, as it must have drained into the river.

Everyone stood shocked, staring at the remains of what was once a human being. "What the hell?" Matt said, breaking the silence.

"We found this stuck in the river grass about a quarter mile up. Nothing else. We searched in all directions. I can tell you the hackles rose on my spine. Must be a fucking big gator out there. I'm not going back in without a spear gun. Poor Jacko....he's gotta be dead, sir."

"What the hell is in this river? Matt asked, turning to Patti.

"We used to have lots of gators and fish, but this year the river life seems to have vanished, aside from an explosion in the minnow population. Maybe the gators are returning."

"I didn't see a gator," the lone diver interjected, A gator big enough to take that leg would have been spotted. I'm telling you, there was nothing there, just river bottom kicked up. So what the hell did this? I marked a waypoint on my GPS. They have it," he said, nodding to the returned divers who were now changing from their diving suits.

"Well, Christ," Matt said. "Maybe you wouldn't have seen it if it was quick enough. Granted, it doesn't make much sense."

"That's one reason Ted was continuously checking the water here, to determine what happened to the river life in this area," Patti said.

"What the hell else could have done this? There's nothing out there capable of this damage besides a huge gator."

"Time's wasting," Monroe said. We have two missing people now, so instead of standing here scratching our heads let's get upriver fast since that's where the leg was found. We have to look for Jack first. He may be alive somewhere on the riverbank, and we can't waste a minute more."

The sheriff gave Matt the directions to the next river access and the divers quickly gathered gear and disappeared into their van. The sheriff and Deputy Dave meticulously retrieved and secured the severed leg and placed it into a plastic evidence bag and into the trunk of the sheriff's car. "We'll get this right off to forensics."

Patti climbed into the back seat of the police car shuddering at the thought of the severed leg behind her in the trunk. *Could have been Ted's leg.* She admonished herself for being grateful that someone else besides Ted had so terrifyingly lost a leg, but it was human nature to be glad it didn't belong to him. The entire scenario was a nightmare; something didn't measure up, but she couldn't put a finger on it. *The bite,* she thought. *No gators for nearly a year...was this Ted's fate, too?* She fought back tears for fear Sheriff Monroe would send her home. She needed to be strong, to be *here*; she needed to be involved. She couldn't show herself a teary female. In order to participate in finding Ted, she had to hold herself together. He would have done the same for her. He would not have given up, or given in to this creeping horror.

"How soon do you think we'll hear from forensics," she asked.

"Don't know, Patti. I'll put a rush on it." Sheriff Monroe backed the car away from the river. A mile down the road they came to another muddy river access. Both vehicles pulled in as far as they could without getting stuck. Recent rains had made a mess of things, which was not a conducive atmosphere for the work they had cut out for themselves.

Again, the divers set off with fresh tanks, and simultaneously the Sheriff, Matt, Deputy Dave and safety divers searched along the river bank for any sign or clue to the missing diver.

Patti stood onshore alone watching the water for any activity. The air was heavy, the humidity clinging to skin and clothing like leeches. She removed her visor a moment to fan her face and armpits. As she turned to retrieve her bottle of water from the sheriff's car, something caught her eye downriver. A flash, a spark of afternoon sun reflecting off an object that appeared briefly and then disappeared, leaving a circular ripple that spread until an edge of its circumference practically reached the shore where she stood.

Gator? Whatever it was, it had surfaced and submerged so quickly that she couldn't register its shape. "Come on back!" she said aloud and, as if on cue, it rose again. This time three very large spikes broke the surface, catching the sunlight. She stepped forward, squinting, wishing she had binoculars, for it was a very peculiar object. The spikes that projected from the water were similar to the osteoderms— the spikes that form on an alligator hide— and yet they were incredibly large. *Largest gator I ever saw,* she thought running the 15 or so feet to the car to grab her cell phone from her purse. Running back, the spikes still peaked through the water's surface, and she zoomed and snapped the lens, then snapped again.

"Sheriff!" she yelled. Something's out there, something huge!"

At the sound of her voice, the spikes moved, turning toward shore and slowly approached. She stepped backward, as now more spikes surfaced, green and brown, mottled and....*and strange.* Her skin prickled in alarm. "Sheriff!" she screamed, as the spiked creature drifted closer. "Gator! *Big* gator! Hurry!"

Somewhere in the distance she heard Sheriff Monroe call to her and felt relief that the men were returning.

"Hurry!" she yelled, as the creature was now a mere twenty to thirty feet offshore. The river floor would now gently rise to the bank, creating a very easy access for an alligator to approach at a good clip. *But it isn't a gator,* she realized with a quickening terror. More spikes rose out of the water and not in the angular shape of an alligator, but a rounder shape, very wide and peaked. In the few seconds she stood mesmerized by the mysterious creature, she could not compute its identity—she, the marine biologist! She, who had hour upon hour of deep sea diving, lake *and* river dives. She simply *could not name the creature.*

"What the...?" Sheriff Monroe stood behind her now.

"My God!" Matt exclaimed beneath his breath. "What is it?"

The return of the men shook Patti from her hypnotic state, and she began snapping photos of the mysterious creature in rapid succession.

The sight of it was startling enough for Monroe to draw his gun, but the creature submerged, forcing waves of water to beat against the shoreline.

"What the hell was that, Patti?"

"I...I have no clue. It almost looked like gator hide, but it was shaped wrong, not to mention the fact that it's impossible for a gator to reach that size. And, it was roundish. I'll take a good long look at the photos when I get home and see if I can determine what it was."

"Whatever it is, it just might be the answer to what happened to Jack and Ted. Email them to me," the sheriff instructed.

"And to me too," Matt said.

"I will, and I'll email them to Kim Su, one of my colleagues in Charleston. Maybe he can help."

CHAPTER FOUR

Buzz ran thick calloused fingers through his trademark salt and pepper crew cut. After two hours on the river he headed for home, but when he noticed the activity on the opposite shore he tucked the skiff within the low hanging branches of Spanish moss-draped sweet gum, tupelo, willow trees and other vegetation that garnished the river bank. Satisfied that he was sufficiently camouflaged and invisible to the divers, the sheriff, his deputy and the girl—the young woman who had caught his eye since the first bud of her breasts twenty years ago—he watched. Yesterday afternoon, only the young woman and Gus were standing on the bank. Now, Sheriff Monroe, Dave Lee, and a dive team filled the space.

"Damn," he said, shooing away a cloud of mosquitos. Something was happening, and he wondered if it could possibly be Snapper's doing? Just the thought, alone, of Snapper returning to his den, made him weary. He cursed his lot in life; he was Snapper's keeper, thanks to his father who had started it all and bestowed upon him this infernal sentence.

The day before, when Gus asked about the whereabouts of Ted Lane, he was hoping the disappearance wasn't Snapper's doing, but now—now that the police and divers were involved—well, evidence was surely pointing in Snapper's direction.

He continued to watch for the return of the divers who had set off earlier when the sole diver had returned. "If Snapper's out there, you ain't findin' nothin'," he said beneath his breath. But then, just as he was about to head for home, the activity on the opposite shore increased; the divers had returned with an object. He reached for his binoculars and jumped slightly in his seat when his eyes focused on said object. "Damn sloppy!" If this was Snapper's doing, there should not have been a trace left!

* * *

Back in his cabin, Buzz opened the trap door that led to the caverns and the damp, clammy atmosphere of the underworld to which he was cursedly chained. He descended the stairway which was bathed in the light from the kitchen, and weaved through the stalagmites and stalactites that hung from the lower end ceiling of the cavern and sprouted from the damp shiny floor below. The constant and familiar drip-drip-drip —the music of the cavern— reached his ears as he peered ahead into the dark void of the passageway where he and his father had once investigated with great caution. His pa had always referred to the curve in the cavern wall as the "Great-Way," but to Buzz it was the 'gateway to hell and damnation'.

"Where are you, you son-of-a bitch," he called into the darkness. The coolness of the cavern caused him to shudder as he peeked into the darkened curve. Always, he was slightly nervous approaching Snapper's domain. *Never know where the bastard is, or if he's even here.* He aimed his flashlight into the black hole.

His father's primitive electrical system had failed years before, and he had neglected to repair it. What was the use, when sometimes Snapper disappeared for years? "Too much money to run," he told his old pop; *old, shriveled son-of-Satan.* He hated the old man, and found some gratification in the fact that the old guy was helpless; the old man who had changed from the friend he had had in his youth, to the cruel, insensitive bastard he became after his mother was gone. He rejoiced watching him shrink until he was a crumpled up ball of meanness and hate— and *helplessness.* That was the best part; he was helpless, and now he, Buzz Abbot, was master and commander and didn't think twice of whacking the old man across the face once in a while just to remind him. "I'm boss now, and don't you forget it," he'd say, and Elmer's gray, watery eyes widened in fear and sometimes even a tear rolled down his cheek. Oh yes, Buzz liked this state of affairs very much.

Then, a familiar shuffling in the deep, dark depths of the Great Way echoed through the void. The offensive odor of the beast filled his

nostrils. Buzz turned and walked quickly back toward the steps, carefully weaving through the damp and shiny teeth of the cavern. Snapper
was back; there would be hell to pay.

CHAPTER FIVE

"We have no further clues, Patti." Sheriff Monroe said over the phone. "We can only leave this an open case and hope Ted shows up. We're waiting for forensics on the diver's leg, and maybe they can tell us what attacked him."

"But you know, and I know, that Ted would never pull something like this on purpose."

"I know, you know, and we all know, but stranger things have happened. Deputy Dave continues to monitor the house and we're investigating friends and acquaintances. That's all we can do."

After an exhausting two full days of river diving, the search was called off. Aside from the severed leg, there was not a trace of either the diver, Jack, or of Ted. The strange creature had not returned. There were no answers to two persons gone missing.

"Crap," she said, shutting off her phone. Her nerves were stretched to the gills. She plopped into a kitchen chair and stared out the small window over the sink. *I can't sit here doing nothing. Something is very wrong and I won't give up!*

With that thought, she rang the Sheriff's office back asking for the number of the dive team captain, Matt. She called him and arranged a meeting at a diner in his town 30 minutes away, the following day.

* * *

He sat across from her, a coffee mug raised to his lips, a pen in hand which he tapped on the table top. He wore no wedding ring. Why on earth she noticed that particularity about him she didn't know. Perhaps it brought to mind Ted and the wedding ring that she would never wear.

"Miss Tripp," he said, setting his mug on the table. "I understand your bereavement and your desire to further investigate the river, but we've completely covered the targeted area. Police have been notified up and down the river that two persons are missing. We can only hope that bod…I'm sorry…something shows eventually."

"I can't give up Mr…Mr…"

"Just call me 'Matt'. Last name's hard to pronounce."

"Okay, Matt. I can't give up. Ted and I were to be married next week. This is devastating, and…" she fought back the urge to cry. "Something's happened to him, and it happened in the river. I hate to think his disappearance—and the killing of your diver—had anything to do with that strange thing we saw, but I can't just stop looking. He *never* would have stopped looking for me." A sob and hiccup followed. She grabbed a napkin from the holder and covered her eyes.

"I'm so sorry," he said, reaching across the table to touch her elbow.

"I know you've done everything you think you can, but it's not enough. I'm going to dive, and I need someone to dive with me. Please find me someone! Please help me!"

He was quiet a moment, staring out the window to the parking lot while she sat nervously twisting the napkin in her hands. "I'm a good diver—lots of hours. I'm a marine biologist, for Pete's sake."

"That strange creature we saw…well, that thing—whatever it is—is still in there. That fact alone doesn't make me eager to send anyone back in there until we find out what it is. Any ideas yet?"

"I'm in contact with Kim Su, as I mentioned. He has the photos but neither of us has come up with a substantial conclusion of what it was. The photos are vague and not very sharp since I snapped them quickly and probably didn't hold my hands still. I wanted to capture it before it submerged. I've also taken into consideration the fact that there is the possibility of an unknown creature in the river, but that idea is unrealistic. There has never been a report of a strange river sighting—none that correlates with what we saw last week. I'm just as anxious to find out what that creature is, but I still have to look for Ted. There is no other place he or your diver could be, except in the river. Why are we turning our backs on them?"

"We're not. Jack's wife and kids are just as distraught. They would like to know what happened to him as well." He again reached across the table, but this time he held out his hand. "I'll go with you, but let's have a plan. Shake on it."

She complied eagerly, a wide smile breaking across her face. "Thanks...thanks so much!"

* * *

She woke in a cold sweat. Fear hugged like a second skin. Goosebumps crawled across her flesh, and her breath came hard and fast. *A dream...it was a dream.* She sat, the covers clutched to her chin, trying to focus her eyes in the darkness. She was grateful for the red digital numbers on the clock next to the bed; it made her feel less alone. *What was it?* She tried to hold onto the dream, for it had truly shaken her awake. *Ted...it was Ted...* then, she remembered.

He was in the river—they were *both* in the river— she, watching from a short distance, the current passing over and beneath her horizontal body.

He beckoned to her. *"Help me!"*

She heard his voice, even over the intake of her breath through the regulator, and even though she knew it was impossible that he could speak submerged in the water; he had no dive equipment. He stood in a great dark void that was familiar, but would not register in her mind. She tried to swim to him, but the current began to pull her backward, away from him.

He beckoned frantically now. "Come get me. Hurry!" But the more she kicked her fins to propel forward, the further back she drifted.

With horror, she watched as a red snake-like object appeared within the dark void. At first it wriggled behind him, knee high, but then grew in height as it waved erratically in the current. She pointed to it, and he turned his head to look. It loomed well above him now. When he tried to step out of the void, away from the creature, it quickly wrapped itself around him until he resembled a mummy, *a red mummy.*

All she could see of him were his eyes—eyes wide in terror. She frantically kicked to reach him, but the flow of the river pulled her further and further away until she saw nothing more than the river bottom.

"It was a dream," she said, quite relieved, and flung the covers off and headed to the bathroom. It was 4:35 a.m. and impossible to return to sleep after the nightmare. The dream, though horribly frightening, just further convinced her to search for Ted until he was found—no matter if he were dead or alive. She accepted the dream as a direct message from Ted himself.

* * *

Predawn, she loaded her car with dive equipment and all the necessaries.

Matt arrived at the river with two coffees and a bag of donuts. "Here," he said, holding out a disposable coffee cup. You'll need this. I know I do. But go light on the donuts until after the dive."

They drank their coffees watching dawn transform the dark river to a mass of moving glitter in the early morning sun. The heat was already oppressive, and the dawn streaked in pinks and oranges low on the eastern sky.

"Okay, here's the plan," Matt said, pulling out a graphed paper. I drew this up last night, with coordinates. We're to stay together. I've brought a spear gun," he added. "As long as we don't know what the odd creature was, and considering the disappearance of two men, we need to be armed. That's my motto, 'when in doubt, be prepared.' I don't think either of us relishes the same fate as Jack, and possibly Ted."

She flinched.

"I'm sorry," he said.

Matt brought enough diving equipment for the both of them. Patti was slightly annoyed, as she was most comfortable in her own gear, but she reluctantly agreed to use the full face communication mask and the other gear, considering his equipment was highly technical and allowed them to speak to one another under water. After 30 minutes of checking equipment and running over the plan, they donned their suits and readied to dive.

"Here," he said, handing her the end of a rope. "Clip this around your waist. Considering that Jack and his dive buddy were only 10 feet apart when Jack disappeared, I think we'd better stick together."

She set a waypoint on her GPS so that she could return to the starting point if an emergency arose and the water clouded as the other divers had said. She fervently hoped there would be no emergencies. Together, they submerged

The water was cool and the current surprisingly strong as they swam against it through the murky river. It reminded her of the dream—the nightmare—in which Ted desperately needed her help. *Not a good place to die.* She was lost in her thoughts and, aside from the sound of her breathing, the silence that came with the underwater world. *No fish,* she observed. *No gators. Just minnows and my breath in the regulator.*

They swam silently tethered together by the umbilical rope, he checking his GPS, and she glancing often in his direction, simply to convince herself that he was still there and had not been carried off by the unknown creature, or, that he was not missing any appendages as was the unfortunate diver, Jack

"Here's where they found Jack's leg," he said, pointing to a patch of river grass, thick and murky, swaying downriver with the current.

She nodded, remembering with vivid accuracy the diver's return with the dismembered leg. Her skin crawled beneath the wetsuit as she thought of the spikes on the strange creature that broke through the surface of the water that day. *It's still here—somewhere.* She continuously scanned the surrounding area as they swam.

Their plan was to swim upriver, and after perusing the stretch closer to shore, to swim further toward the middle of the river on the return. After a rest and a change of tanks, they would continue with the middle river upward, and back again to home base while covering the waters closer to the opposite shore.

The nakedness, the emptiness of the river was astounding. Surely there should be turtles, bass and other river life aplenty, but, aside from the minnows, it was as void of life as the moon. Nothing stirred—*nothing*—until a cloud of brown, churning river bottom as thick as a wall of brick forged through the water toward them.

"Stop!" Matt said, and she did, both staring wide-eyed at the clouded mass. "Let's go!" he said, indicating the direction of the shore; but just as they headed to escape the mysterious mass, the clouded mass sucked them into its blinding hold. With the river now churned into the current, she lost her bearing. When she felt a pull on the rope she panicked before realizing it was Matt, tugging her toward him. Hand over hand on the rope she closed the distance between them. Her heart thumped wildly in her chest as she tried to maintain a semblance of calm, but visions of the strange peaks that appeared to her in the river after Ted's disappearance played through her mind. *Monster? Is it behind us?* Within moments they felt the river bottom beneath them and feeling somewhat safer, Patti stopped the frantic swim and turned; *nothing but muddy water.* The wall of muck was dispersing, but not before she caught a glimpse of something long, ridged, tapered to a sharp point—something familiar, yet vague—dragging along the bottom and disappearing into the foggy remains of the blinding brown cloud.

"What the heck?" she said, removing her equipment once they were safely (she hoped) on shore.

"I don't know," Matt replied, removing his own vest and mask.

They sat on the bank, further upstream than where they had begun their search.

"Look at me," she said, holding trembling hands out for his observance. "I'm shaking! What was that thing? Did you see a tail—or something like a tail—drag along the bottom?"

"Sure did."

"I feel like I should know what it is. It's familiar, but it was so *big*…." Her mind fought desperately to place the thick, tapered object, but it didn't register into any category of aquatic life that she could readily place…*or did it?* It was the size— the amazing size— of the thing that baffled her.

* * *

"Oh my God!" She shot straight up in bed. "Oh, my God!" she repeated, and grabbed the phone, glancing once at the digital time display on the radio; 4:25 a.m. She touched #8 on speed dial.

"Wha....? Who is this?" The gravelly voice on the other end of the phone did not sound happy. "This better be damned important. Do know what time it is?"

"Matt!"

"Yeah? Who is this? What's wrong?"

"It's me, Patti. Sorry to wake you, but I know what it is, Matt. it came to me while I was sleeping."

"What came to you?"

"That long tapered tail, I know this sounds crazy—impossible, even—but I'm certain that thing is a turtle, and a big one."

"You're right, it *is* insane. Go back to sleep. Turtles don't get that large. I saw it too, you know. It's impossible. You had a nightmare." She had his full and quite irritated attention now.

"I know, I know. It's insane, but it all makes sense. The spikes in the river, the rounder shape of the body—it was *the shell* that I saw that day, Matt; the carapace of a turtle. The spikes were osteoderms, and the only turtle that has a shell like that is the Alligator Snapping Turtle. It all fits."

"This is crazy."

CHAPTER SIX

Riverside, Georgia
1937

Elmer Abbot was quite excited. His pa let him put the turtle, a fine yet strange specimen, in Ma's washtub complete with a rock to climb on. Ma wasn't happy, but Pa promised to buy her a new tub in town.

"Ugly as all get-out," Pa said when Elmer showed up with the creature, which he held pinched between his fingers, as it was surprisingly vicious for such a small thing.

Ma agreed; it was a very ugly turtle.

"Found him by the river, Pa. He tried to bite me, but I ain't never seen one like it. Looks kinda like a gator, don't ya think?"

"Yep, it's an alligator snapper, son. He can take your finger right off, so be extra careful. Ain't seen one in a long time."

His pa was smart; he knew everything about all the critters they came across living in the woods, and all the critters in the river. Pa was kind, too; he understood Elmer's love of all critters and encouraged him to learn all he could about the world in which he lived.

It was the height of the Great Depression. Pa was a good hunter and kept the family well fed with game he shot or trapped himself. He trapped raccoon, possum and other creatures of the forest, and cured the pelts in hopes that one day people would have money to buy them. The family was well sustained, and they never starved. Ma kept a patch of garden out back in the only square of sunshine that managed to shine through the tall and thick vegetation of the forest. She grew cabbage and collards in the colder months, lots of squash in the summer, tomatoes and melons too. Green pole beans and peas climbed their way up the wooden fence posts and chicken wire that Pa put up to keep the deer away. They ate well enough to stay healthy, and when they had an abundance of produce, she took it to the farmer's market in town hoping the townsfolk had enough money to buy.

Elmer learned his letters from Ma. So many kids had to drop out of school to find work to help feed their families that it was hardly worth attending. Perhaps when things got better, he would go back to school with a real teacher. Elmer didn't like sitting still for lessons; he loved exploring the forest, the river and all that flourished there. At eleven years of age, he pretty much made up his mind that he would never leave the river, the woods, and the home he loved.

* * *

1942

"Dang it, son. Snappers gettin' too big. You gotta let him go soon."

Elmer, now 16 years of age, tall and muscular, held a thick six inch strip of red meat over Snapper's head. The turtle now lived in a ten foot oblong pool, hand dug and cemented by Elmer two years past. Snapper was privy to nearly four feet of walking space around his pool, as well as four feet of water in which he spent most of his time. Snapper, himself, was a good three feet in length, not including his head, neck and tail.

"This is a swimmin' turtle. He needs the river and needs to learn how to catch his own food." Pa said, jumping back when Snapper leapt for the piece of meat, his neck extended, jaws snapping shut alarmingly quick and hard over the food.

"Hot damn, that guy can jump! Did you see how long his neck is?" Elmer wiped his hands on the sides of his jeans. Snapper never failed to amaze him.

"I never knew no turtle to jump, Elm. I got a creepy feeling about this guy, and your Ma does too. You gotta let him go."

"Are you serious? I can't let him go, Pa! He's my friend, my pal, my—he's like a part of me."

"Sooner or later, Snapper's gonna want a mate. If it's anything like any other animal in season, it ain't gonna be pretty if you have him penned up like this."

* * *

1953

Elmer returned from service at the end of the Korean War, to Jane, his wife, whom he married before the war, and a two-year-old son, Buzz, whom he had never met. Elmer proved a good soldier during the war years, adept as he was at living in a semi-wilderness and his expertise in handling firearms. On his return, with Ma now passed away and Pa growing older, a good portion of the maintenance of the home place fell upon his and Jane's shoulders

Snapper's pen and pool had been enlarged several times in the years before Elmer was drafted. After the war, what originally began as a small chicken wire pen had grown into a 25' by 25' chain-link compound complete with a deep hibernation pool dug with Old Pa's rusty old backhoe. Money was tight during the war years, but enough had been saved between what Elmer sent home and Jane's job in town as a cashier in a grocery store to keep Snapper in a strong compound and fed with fresh game, and often fish from the river.

"I swear, Elmer Abbot, you love that beast more than you love me." Jane was certain this was true. Life revolved around maintaining Snapper; but no matter how much Jane and Old Pa complained, Elmer was not about to give up his old friend.

"Ain't no way in the world I could love anything more'n I love you, Janie girl." He lifted her with his muscular arms and twirled her around the kitchen.

"Put me down, silly," she said, an onion in one hand, a dish-towel in the other.

"You know I love you best of all." He trapped her between his arms at the kitchen sink and nuzzled her neck. "Well, maybe I do love Snapper a smidgeon more'n you..."

* * *

1965

"Pa! Pa!" Buzz entered the kitchen, his face red and shiny with sweat. Snapper's dinner, three dead rabbits, dangled from his belt. "Where's Pa? Snappers *gone*; he's *gone!*"

Jane dropped a jar of canned tomatoes. It bump- bump- bumped across the uneven planks of the kitchen floor and dipped into the slope beneath the table. She steadied herself against the sink, her eyes staring beyond the screen door. "Good Lord, if that don't send shivers up my spine, I don't know what will. Pa's out back. Go fetch him, and hurry!"

"I warned him," said Old Pa as he slowly pushed his walker toward the table. "Dang thing got so big he don't dare let him go. Can't set somethin' like that free into the river. Why, he'd eat up every bit o' life in it!"

"I never liked that thing; it ain't natural." Jane pulled a chair out from the table and retrieved the jar, which had blessedly not broken on impact. "Will you just look at this dip in the floor? I keep telling Elm to fix this floor, but he ain't done it yet. Guess he's waiting for it to cave in. Then what? Then he'll have twice the work! Sit down, Old Pa. I'll fix you a plate. Who knows when Elm will come in for supper now that Snapper is out there, somewhere."

Old Pa settled his thin and frail body onto the chair. "I told him to let Snapper go years ago when he was at a natural size, but he couldn't give him up, and now it's too late—he's let his own self go."

"I ain't stepping out this door till they find him." Jane said with a shudder.

* * *

Elmer stared at the gaping hole in the compound fence, which was now expanded to 30' by 30' feet and had required cutting down some of the surrounding trees to make room. Buzz stood wide-eyed beside him.

"Damn." he said, searching the perimeter of the clearing, his eyes settling on the odd tracks in the dirt. "Well, son, he went this way. Let's go."

Buzz removed the rabbits from his belt and took them to the kitchen. "Should I bring the rifle?" he yelled from behind the screen door.

"Hell, no. I ain't killing my best friend."

Father and son followed the telltale tracks left by the drag of Snapper's tail. They followed the odd swath across the dirt, across the flattened brush and broken branches created by Snapper's heavy and immense body, until they reached the river, where the trail ended.

"What now, Pa?"

Elmer looked up, down, and across the river, seeing nothing unusual. He wanted to cry, but couldn't do so—*wouldn't* do so— in front of Buzz. He had to be a man and set a good example for the boy. Later, after supper, after all went to bed, Elmer lit a lantern and followed the path to the river. There, he sat on the bank in the dark and sobbed.

CHAPTER SEVEN

1966

"You're crazy, Elm," Jane said nearly a year later. "I think you miss Snapper more than you'd miss me if I was gone."

Elmer shrugged, as he stood at Snapper's old compound, ready to pull it down. "Can't help that I miss him; I had him most of my life."

"You waited long enough, and he ain't comin' back," she said, disappearing into the cabin with a basket full of dry laundry. "And a good riddance!" she called from the cabin. "He wasn't like a normal turtle and you know it. No turtle gets that big and nasty."

Nearly every day Elmer stood on the banks of the river, his eyes traveling up and downstream, hoping to catch a glimpse of his old friend. Once, he got his hopes up when a row of osteoderms surfaced, but they were small and in an angular shape; *a gator, just a young gator.* He hadn't seen a gator in quite a while, which was odd, but he had his suspicions.

On this particular evening, when the family sat for the evening meal at the kitchen table—a table worn and dented from decades of use by the Abbot family— a strange sound reached their ears.

"Did you hear that, Jane?"

"I did. Where's it coming from?"

"What?" Old Pa yelled, his hearing having ebbed away with his advancing age.

"Shush." Elmer held a finger to his lips, and the family held their breaths in unison, listening.

The strange sound returned, only louder, and with it a slight tremor of the kitchen floor.

"Oh!" Jane squealed. "We're having an earthquake!"

"What?" Old Pa asked.

"Get out of the kitchen!" Elmer yelled, as the sound grew even louder beneath them.

Everyone scooted, except for Old Pa who was so thin that Elmer lifted him effortlessly and removed him to the small living room. After setting him on the sofa he returned to stand in the kitchen doorway, his eyes wide as pieces of the floor broke and fell into an ever widening dark hole.

"What is it, Elm?" Jane asked, her breath warm on his back.

"I don't know—get back, Jane!" He pushed her away and stared in awe at the gaping hole and the echoing sounds of broken floorboards hitting a hard surface. "My God," he whispered. "What's happening?"

The hole widened even more, and the old table lost its footing as one leg disappeared into the dark pit, leading the rest of the table– and dinner–into the abyss with the resounding crash of silverware, plates, and the table itself.

"There's a bottom to it," Elmer said aloud, as the chairs followed the table one by one. Old Pa's walker followed suit, its metal clanking at the end of its journey into the dark pit.

After what seemed an eternity, all was still. Elmer gingerly made his way to the large hole, testing the floorboards as he went and making sure to only move over the remaining support beams. He peered into the abyss, but it was too dark to make anything of it; it was just a black hole. As he bent to peer into the pit, an atmosphere of foul humidity and dampness wafted from the bowels of the mysterious hole, enveloping his face, and filling the kitchen.

"Come with me, Buzz," he said, returning to the living room. "We need a ladder, lanterns, flashlights and rope."

"You're not going down there, are you?" Jane asked, alarmed.

"Of course! How else will I know what's happened?"

"What if the whole cabin caves in?" she cried. "Should we go outside?"

"Calm down woman, I gotta look."

"What's happening?" Old Pa demanded.

"It's okay," Elmer yelled. "Keep calm!"

"What's happening?" Old Pa repeated.

"Don't go!" Jane pleaded.

"Hush up, woman. Calm yourself and don't upset Old Pa."

* * *

Armed with a lantern and flashlight, father and son climbed the full extent of the 12 foot ladder downward into the mysterious pit of darkness. Once standing on solid but stony wet ground, Elm held the lantern` outward, making a circular sweep of their surroundings and stood speechless, eyes wide open.

"My god," he whispered.

"Has this always been here?"

"...a cavern. I had no idea...."

"Where does it go?" Buzz made a sweep with the flashlight. "Look at them daggers!" Indeed, practically at eye level, stalactites hung like jagged teeth from the uneven, rutted ceiling of the cavern, while stalagmites rose before them from the wet cavern floor like an army of swords ready to impale

The men made a path through the debris left from the kitchen; chairs, walker, wood, broken plates, silverware and their meal, literally lay scattered before them. They weaved through the eerie stalactite and stalagmites, walking further into the unknown darkness, Elmer holding out the lantern, while Buzz shined the flashlight ahead to guide their footsteps. The humid dankness of the cavern enveloped them as they proceeded cautiously forward.

"What are these things called?" Buzz asked, gingerly touching the tip of a four foot cone.

"Sta...Stalac...I can't remember the name—them things that grow in caverns. I never knew this was here." Elmer shook his head in wonder.

A faint *drip... drip... drip* echoed from somewhere in the cavern, as well as the sound of running water.

"Sounds like a river, Pa, but where's it coming from?"

"I...what was that?"

"What?"

"Shush... listen...."

Somewhere in the dark cavern a dull thud followed by splashing water caught their attention.

"I hear it," Buzz whispered. "What is it?"

"Sounds like somebody dragging something. Wait."

Again, the sound reached their ears, followed by a quickened scraping.

"What is that? This is creepy."

"Shush." Elmer held his lantern outward in the direction of the sound. He stepped forward, while Buzz hung back, one foot ready to turn and run.

"Who goes?" Elmer called.

The scraping became quicker, louder; it was approaching, and *fast*. Elmer did full circle with the lantern. "Dang, can't tell where it's coming from."

Three distinct hisses now rang through the mysterious chamber. Elmer held the lantern in the direction from which he thought he heard the sounds. The light filtered through a slew of longer stalactites, as the ceiling had gained height from the entrance of the kitchen to this point. The light focused on a cavern wall, curved and shiny with moisture. There appeared to be a bend, a passageway, darkened and out of view beyond the perimeter of the lantern's light. Elmer looked behind to the way they had come. A faint light from the hole in the kitchen floor was their marker for the return, and he had kept it in sight during the sojourn in the cave. He stepped backward, feeling the hairs on his neck raise as more scrapes and hisses echoed through the yet unseen dark corridors.

"Let's go, Pa, it's getting closer!"

Elm again shined the light against the cavern wall at the bend, certain now that whatever was approaching, was traveling through the dark passage. He stepped backward again, his eyes glued on the dark curvature of the cavern wall.

"Look!" Buzz yelled.

With horror, Elm's eyes focused at the shadow on the wall, a huge creature, spiked like the stalagmites that rose from the floor. He shook his head, and focused again. The black shadow now twisted, grotesquely changing as it rounded the bend.

"Snapper!" Buzz yelled before his father could register what he saw;

Snapper? A microsecond of jubilation at the reunion with his pet soon turned to a race for life. Snapper eyed the men, hissed and exhaled, sending a horrid blast of foul air in the direction of his trespassers. His exceedingly long and sharpened claws scraped at the cavern floor as he picked up speed, his pointed knife-like upper and lower beaks snapping as he approached.

"Get to the ladder!" Elmer yelled, but it was difficult to make speed. As in a dream, the lighted guiding point of the hole in the kitchen floor seemed further away the faster they tried to approach. First, they had to maneuver the stalactites and stalagmites making it necessary to duck and weave their way through the maze. Then the barricades became the food, chairs, table, and all that fell through the mysterious hole in the kitchen floor.

All the while, Snapper's claws scrapped menacingly on the limestone floor as he approached his fleeing prey. Closer and closer it came until two loud crashes, one after the other, caused Elmer to turn and look. Snapper was stopped in his tracks! The ceiling narrowed to a point where the ominous teeth of the cave blocked his ability to follow further without breaking off dozens more than the two stalactites and stalagmites that rolled down a slope in the cavern floor. They were heavy, as indicated by the thuds of their rolling and thumping until they hit the cavern wall at the bend. Snapper hissed, his sharp beak chomping at air as he viewed the trespassers safely caged behind the lower hanging stalactites.

"Hurry!" Elmer yelled. "Up the ladder!"

* * *

"*Snapper?* Snapper is down there?" Jane was bewildered. It was a day of days; the collapsing of the kitchen floor, and now the reappearance of Snapper, angry and living below.

"I'm telling you, Jane, he's grown—huge! Big and mean, that's what he is. His claws are big as daggers, and that beak of his, why he was snappin' at us and *hissin'* even. He was trying to kill us, Jane! You'd think after all the care I done for him, after all the years together, that he'd remember me—know who I am—but he don't."

"He was so scary, Ma! He was big as this house, I swear... and chomping his beak at us!"

The entire family, including Old Pa, sat outside on porch chairs which had been brought into the yard for safety purposes in case the rest of the house decided to collapse beneath them.

"What's that?" Old Pa piped in. You talkin' about that turtle o' yours?"

"Yes," Elm yelled. "Snapper—he's living in a cavern. There's a damn cavern below us!"

"Why are we out here?" Old Pa asked. "I wanna go to bed."

Elmer rested his forehead in his palms, elbows on knees. "What now?"

"I'm not sleeping in that house, Elm. Why, I'll be up all night waiting for it to fall in like the kitchen."

Elmer looked at the old homestead. It appeared to have nothing wrong from the outside—no holes like the one in the kitchen, at any rate—but something had to be done. They couldn't live outdoors and they couldn't afford to move to town, and didn't want to move in the first place; they were river people, this land was home. He'd have to fix the cabin, that's what. He'd fix it from below; brace it, make it strong so they'd never have a floor collapse beneath them again.

Because the cabin appeared to have been built over the lesser depth of the cavern, it would be much easier to brace than had it been over an area of twenty to even thirty or forty feet in height. Elmer could not examine the rest of cavern as he'd like, because of the danger of encountering Snapper. First, he had to brace the house. Second, he had to figure out what to do with his old pet that had now become a dangerous menace.

* * *

As it was summertime and Buzz was out of school, the bracing of the cabin from beneath began immediately. First, the area around the hole in the kitchen floor was braced with timber cut from surrounding felled trees. When the timbers were set, the hole was framed, and covered with a trap door for convenient access. A stairway was constructed and after that, a generator was set to run a primitive electrical wiring system from which hung light bulbs stationed throughout the construction area, strung from strategically spaced timber poles within the safety area. Elmer and Buzz were grateful for the stalactites and stalagmites that kept Snapper at bay, for he was attracted by the sounds of construction that echoed throughout the cavern, and he sometimes came to watch.

He was a terrifying sight, enhanced not only by his abnormal size and height, but by the algae that grew across his shell and hung in ragged, smelly clumps; a mangy dinosaur, misplaced by some twist of genetic fate and now here, a living nightmare; powerful, hideous—a beast to be reckoned with.

He had grown from the time of his escape. Previously, his shell was approximately four feet in length, his height at three to four feet, his tail another three feet when extended, his head another two. His width at that time, with feet and claws extended, along with a neck that stretched at least two more feet, made his figure quite formidable. Now, it appeared to Elmer that he had grown twice-fold since he vanished, but how?

The unnerving way Snapper watched the two men work from behind the natural barricade of stalactites and stalagmites intimidated them. As they moved from place to place within their compound, so did Snapper in his own realm of the underworld. His foul breath mixed with the damp air and permeated their space. The scuffling of his immense body, the scratching of his claws, the beady black eyes set in the lumbering head, it was enough to keep them ever mindful that Snapper watched and waited.

From a maze of beams and metal came a construction that would stand strong, should another sinkhole occur. Elmer scoured the town dump, back alley trash, and any other place where he thought he could find discarded metal and wood. Every penny that could be spared went into the purchase of supplies for the support structure. Ma's garden was needed now more than ever before, and she tended it with care. Canned goods from years past disappeared rapidly from the pantry shelves. Hunting squirrel, possum, muskrat, deer and rabbit was essential for their consumption. By the fall of 1966 the home place was secure. In the event that the sinkhole would further expand, the cabin would stand as strong as a house on stilts of steel at the edge of an angry sea.

CHAPTER EIGHT

1970

"I don't smell him," Buzz said, continuing to sniff the air at the bottom of the steps. The hanging light bulbs made it quite possible for Buzz and his father to see Snapper when he approached; but best of all, the gagging odors of algae, moss and decaying mud that clung to the misbegotten giant, preceded him in warning.

"Let's go," Elmer said, holding a propane lantern ahead as they made their way through the teeth of the cave, the stalactites and stalagmites that were their protection. "Let's check the Great Way and make sure he's not coming."

Since the building of the bracing structure for the cabin above, they had installed galvanized steel pipes at four foot intervals in a semi-circle, allowing them approximately fifteen feet at the widest part of the semi-circle from the bottom of the stairway to Snapper's domain. The pipes were attached into the cavern floor with post holes jackhammered and filled with cement. It was impossible to attach all of them to the ceiling, but some stood high enough to secure themselves between the cracks and crevices of the lower parts of the cavern ceiling. They held fast, thus discouraging Snapper from crossing the line.

Foot by foot the men attempted to investigate the rest of the cavern by extending the electrical wiring. This could only be done when Snapper was not present, but they had their secure semi-circle to run to should Snapper approach.

A year prior, they had finally discovered what lay beyond the bend in the wall. Their first view with lantern and flashlight did not unveil the eerie beauty of the cavern. It was not until they strung and lit the last two and newest bulbs on the electrical wire that stretched from the kitchen to this place that they stood in awe and wonder at the magnificence of their surroundings; it took their breath away. The cavern exploded into an immense colorful underworld of stalactites and stalagmites several feet longer, higher, heavier and wider than the ones that formed on the cavern ceiling and floor beneath the kitchen. They hung from the ceiling as mystical teeth of an unearthly yet gorgeous creature welcoming them with mouth wide open. They sprang from the damp cavern floor as fantastical jutting spikes and spears, creating a seemingly endless underground labyrinth of danger and enchantment; and it was then that Elmer dubbed the chamber the "Great Way".

They walked alongside the river hoping this time to discover where it entered into the main river, for it must enter somewhere. The bank alongside the water way left approximately three dry feet on which the men could walk. As for Snapper, he would have to approach against the underground river current in this way. As the electrical lighting diminished leaving only the visibility of the lantern and flashlight, they proceeded cautiously, always sniffing the air for the scent of Snapper.

"You'd think we'd see light ahead somewhere." Buzz said. "Ain't nothin' but black as far as I can tell, which ain't far." The flashlight flickered. "Damn." He gave it a shake. It lit a moment and then went completely dark.

"I hope you have extra batteries in your pocket, boy." Elmer said as he continued ahead, the lantern glowing in the foreground.

Buzz felt his pockets, but they lay flat. "Oh, oh, Pa."

"Dang it, Buzz! This ain't the place to be unprepared!"

"Sorry, Pa. Guess we'd better turn back."

"I still got lots of juice in the lantern. Let's go further. Maybe we'll get lucky today."

Buzz stuffed the flashlight into his jeans pocket and followed closely behind his father. As they proceeded, he began to feel apprehensive. "Maybe we should go back, Pa. It feels creepy this far in." The Great Way had totally disappeared behind them. Should the lantern go out, they would be stranded in total darkness; but Pa continued walking the narrow bank alongside the river, slowly following its gentle twists and turns.

"How far do you think we've gone?" Buzz asked.

"Half a mile, maybe. Don't really know. It's hard to tell down here." Elmer stopped suddenly and sniffed, then sniffed again. "We may have trouble, boy."

Buzz's skin prickled. He sniffed at the dank air. "Shit," he whispered "He's here. Let's go—hurry!"

"Shhh." Elmer warned. Elmer moved to the front with the lantern, leaving Buzz to continuously glance behind as they walked quickly, hoping to see the lights from the Great Way.

As the river's depth grew shallower the further into the cave, the sounds of Snapper approaching soon caught up with the horrendous odor that had preceded his arrival. The men made their way as quietly as was humanly possible, so as not to alert the beast of their existence. Soon, though, Snapper's odor filled the passage with such overpowering stench that Buzz was fairly near to panic. "Hurry up, Pa, he's getting closer!" he whispered.

At last, a dim glow ahead announced their approach to the Great Way and electrical lighting. They hurried now, and so much so that Elmer's lantern clipped a small and spindly stalagmite and broke it off, sending it crashing to the cavern floor. "Damn!"

After a moment of silence in the passage, the quickening sound of Snapper running through the riverbed hastened their speed. There was no doubt about it now. *Snapper knew.*

"Christ, Pa, he'll get us!"

They scurried, tripping, glancing back while racing to the Great Way and the passage to safety.

"He's here!" Buzz yelled, horrified. There was no need to whisper at this point, as the snapping of the powerful, sharp beak was closer than ever.

Elmer halted abruptly and turned. "Stop!" he yelled at the scraggly, stinking mess of a monster barreling toward him. He waived his arms, the lantern bobbing erratically, but Snapper paid no mind. "Run, Buzz!"

"Not without you!" Buzz replied, standing next to his father, attempting to scare off the beast, but it was no use; Snapper continued toward them, his thick, clawed feet seeming to float across the cavern floor at high speed. "He ain't stoppin'— let's go!" Buzz yelled.

Elmer swung the lantern and let it fly at the beast, hitting Snapper square on the beak. It fell to the ground, breaking apart, spreading a pool of burning oil. Snapper nearly screeched at the burst of flames that singed his forefeet and neck, but quickly sidestepped, continuing the chase. His dagger-like claws scraped against the moist stone floor in horrifying clarity. As he narrowed the distance between him and his prey—so close—the men felt the exhale of his putrid breath on their necks. They raced through the Great Way, hearts pumping, gasping for air and finally reaching the curvature that led to their own domain.

* * *

Jane cocked her head to the side having heard hollering from below. She knew Elmer and Buzz were down there, but they had never actually yelled before, but...*there it is again.* She hunched by the trap door and peered beyond the staircase, but could see nothing but the immediate cave floor that dully shined from the light of the string of bulbs. Only once had she ventured down the stairs and that was because Buzz and Elmer insisted that she see Snapper's new appearance. Once was enough; he was as terrifying to her as he always had been, only now, he was much, *much* larger, a true monster.

The yells became louder, which alarmed her to the extent of taking the staircase down to stand behind the steel bars anxiously watching the crook in the passageway that curved and led to the Great Way. She had never seen the Great Way and had no intentions of ever doing so.

When Elmer stumbled around the curved corridor, she knew something was seriously wrong.

"What is it?" she screamed, her heart racing. "Where's Buzz?"

"He's comin'!" Elmer muttered breathlessly as he scrambled toward the bars.

Buzz appeared next, but behind him came the most terrifying sight Jane ever hoped to see, the shaggy, smelly, ungodly looking monster right on Buzz's tail!

She shrieked, a piercing sound that boomeranged around the cavern at a deafening pitch. "Buzz! Run!" she screamed. "Elmer, save him!"

Elmer turned to see that Buzz, in his race to safety, had tripped and fallen. He ran fearlessly toward his son and Snapper, howling in defiance of the beast. Snapper had now straddled Buzz, who was struggling—clawing—his way toward the steel bars. Should Snapper misstep, he could impale Buzz with his claws.

As Elmer approached, Snapper swung his great head, hitting Elmer in the chest and sending him flying. He crashed into the wall at the bend and collapsed to the floor.

Jane was desperate to save her son. Without thought, she ran through the steel bars and straight at the beast. Shrieking like a banshee, she jumped and danced in front of his lumbering head, desperate to get his attention.

"Hurry, Buzz, she yelled. "Move!"

"Get back, Ma!" Buzz, now on all fours, crawled quickly through Snapper's front legs. He stood, grabbed his mother's hand and turned to run—but he couldn't move; Snapper, the horrid and ungodly freak of nature, had his mother's arm locked in his beak. "No!" he yelled, pounding the beast's immense beak with his fist. Snapper raised his head, Jane's arm still locked between his jaws, her legs dangling above the cavern floor. He shook her like a dog's toy, she, screaming hysterically as her body jerked dramatically through the air. With one final jerk of Snapper's head, she fell to the ground, her arm severed at the shoulder.

"My God!" Buzz yelled, hauling her up off the floor. "Pa!"

"Look what he's done!" Jane screamed, glancing at the ragged, raw and blood-pumping jagged emptiness that once was her arm.

At this moment, Elmer came to, shaking his head, getting his bearing. What he saw would remain embedded in his mind until death; his beloved Jane, limp in Buzz's arms, bleeding profusely, and Snapper—his pet, his beast from hell—making one final lunge, plucking her from Buzz's arms as precisely as if he were a mother cat plucking a kitten from danger.

Buzz stared in horror at the sight of his mother, now clenched hopelessly and listlessly in the jaws of Snapper, his beak pierced clean through her abdomen. The beast turned, his prize secured, and passed Elmer, who sat dazed and in shock, against the cavern wall.

Surely, this was a dream. Surely, Jane would be up in the kitchen preparing supper. Surely, this had never happened. But it had. The men remained transfixed; Buzz beside a pool of his mother's blood, and Elmer against the wall. Neither spoke. They could only stare at the passage and listen to Snapper as he scuffled his way to wherever…wherever it was he lived, wherever it was he took and finished his prize meals.

* * *

"You could have saved her," Elmer said from the porch chair. It was just about all he said anymore. "You could have saved her and you let her die."

It was not the first time Buzz heard the accusations. Six months had passed since Jane's horrific death, and Buzz was still to blame.

"Not even a burial, a headstone. Nothin'. You let her go for turtle food."

Buzz packed his bags and joined the Army.

CHAPTER NINE

2015

"**D**o you realize how nuts this sounds?"

"We do, Sheriff. It's...well, it's crazy," Matt said, shifting in the hard-backed wooden chair in front of Monroe's desk. Patti sat on an identically worn chair to his right.

"I'll say it's nuts. What am I supposed to do, tell my men we're on the lookout for a giant turtle monster?"

"It's an alligator snapper," Patti said. "And this is not an ordinary turtle. This turtle is extremely large, has razor claws, a razor sharp beak, a nasty disposition and a big appetite. It's an Olympic swimmer, has incredible maneuverability and is as strong as King Kong. It's dangerous enough without becoming jumbo sized."

"Do you think...?" Sheriff Monroe began, and then stopped.

"Do I think this is what got Ted?"

Matt reached out to place a hand on Patti' arm.

"I do," she said, stifling her emotions. "I don't want to believe it, but what else can it be? I think this explains his disappearance, the disappearance of the diver, and probably the young couple who vanished down river recently."

"Good Christ," Monroe mumbled and pressed a button on his phone. "Dave, get in here—on the double."

Within 30 seconds, Deputy Dave filed through the door to stand at Monroe's desk.

"Better grab a chair," Monroe said, nodding to the remaining wooden chair against a wall.

"What's up? Do we have a lead?" Dave asked, dragging the chair across the floor to sit beside Patti.

"Sort of." Monroe began. "Patti and Matt here say that there is a giant turtle living in the river and that it is the cause of Ted and the diver's disappearance…and perhaps the reason we have photos of the missing young couple tacked to the corkboard.

Dave grinned. "Oh come on. Really? What's up?"

"Do you think I would joke about this?" Patti said sharply. "I'm serious. There is a giant Alligator Snapping Turtle in the river, and it's killing people. We've seen it! Get those photos on your computer, Sheriff—the ones I sent you."

"I'm sorry, Patti," Dave said. "I know it's nothing to joke about."

"I already have the photos up. Look." Monroe turned his computer monitor toward the group. "See these bumps here?" Monroe pointed his pen at the mottled peaks breaking the water. "Patti took these shots the day the dive team first searched the river. Patti and Matt say this is an alligator snapper—a very, very *large* snapper." He leaned into the monitor, squinting. "Hmm, I think maybe they have something there, now that I'm looking at the photos. These bumps couldn't belong to an alligator." His pen followed the wide, arched, spiny curvature of the strange object. "Oh boy," he said, setting his pen down. "How could this happen?"

"Believe me, I want to find an answer to that question, too. My colleague, Kim Su, is on his way here."

"No word of this to anyone, Dave, until we have a handle on it," Monroe said.

"Well, hell, who'd believe it anyway? But—what about folks going for a swim? It's hotter'n blazes out there, and you know dang well folks'll be cooling off all the way from Savannah to Athens."

"He has a point," Monroe said. "Why haven't we ever seen this—this thing— before now?"

Patti shrugged. "I have no clue. I'm as mystified as you are."

"We'll put 'no fishing' and 'no swimming' signs within our jurisdiction," Monroe said.

"With what excuse?" Dave asked.

"Unsafe water, that's what, but I'm sure the signs will be over-looked."

"What about outside our jurisdiction?" Patti asked.

"We should alert our bordering counties, but I hate to do that unless I'm dang sure there really is a giant turtle out there. It would help more to convince me if I saw it in person." Monroe shook his head. "This is nuts."

"So far as we know, the creature is staying in this area. Alligator snappers normally don't have dens, and it's too hot out there to hibernate, so where does it go? And I agree, why has no one seen it before?" Patti looked at Matt, who had sat quietly throughout the exchange. "At the moment, this is its hunting ground. We have to find it, Matt."

"I was afraid you'd say that, but you're right. We need to get on it before anyone else disappears.

* * *

Matt arrived at Patti's door that afternoon with a topographical river map rolled up and held in place by one muscular arm. Laying the map out on the kitchen table, they sat with a magnifying glass, a marker, and an orange highlighter.

"This is where we saw the snapper's tail," Matt said, drawing an 'x' with the marker. "And this is where you saw him first." He marked an 'x' where Patti stood the afternoon that the diver had disappeared—the day she first spotted the strange spikes from the riverbank. "This is where the leg was found. Two different days, two different places, but still in this area." He ran a finger up the side of the river in the areas the creature had been spotted. "I guess we start from the beginning."

* * *

Kim Su arrived late that afternoon, suitcase in hand. He stood 5'9", slender bodied, dressed in jeans and a tee shirt with "Nerds are People Too" written in large red letters across the front. Jet black gelled hair stood to a point in the middle of his crown, while beady dark eyes peered from behind black rimmed glasses.

"New do?" Patti asked, suppressing a grin. "Attractive, I'd say."

"I knew you'd love it." Kim replied, setting his suitcase down. "I'm so sorry about Ted." He wrapped his slender arms around her and squeezed.

Patti sighed. "I know, thanks." *Don't cry,* she told herself. *Don't weaken.* "I still have hope, Kim, but not much considering what we've discovered. Circumstances don't point to a favorable outcome. Come on and meet Matt, our dive captain."

With introductions over, the threesome huddled over the topo map while Patti described the river, the sightings and the upcoming hunt.

"This is dangerous work, Kim. Be forewarned." Matt said. "We have to find out where this thing goes, where it lives, and why it's here."

"I'm plenty experienced," Kim said. "An expert diver, like Patti."

"Kim and I work well together," Patti interjected. "We've been dive partners a long time."

"Honestly, I don't like the thought of either of you on this hunt," Matt said. "We know how dangerous it is. I should get a dive team toge...."

"*We're* your dive team, Matt." Patti' heatedly interrupted. "We can't have word of this getting out yet. Who knows what mayhem would follow. We'd probably have every hunter in the state here shooting up the river. It isn't happening; you're stuck with us."

"You have a point there. Okay, I've got my dive team but just remember, *I'm* dive captain. You may be expert in this turtle business, but I'm expert in rescue and recovery. Now I'll add 'underwater investigator,' to that list. We go armed, so I hope you two know how to use spear guns."

"We do," Kim replied. "We've swum with practically every predator in the sea—armed."

"But not this one…" Patti whispered.

* * *

Two days passed before the trio stood riverside where Ted had taken his last swim. Suited and armed, they submerged into water that was murkier and the current stronger than usual, due to a storm that had passed through causing the two-day delay. Untethered they set out up-river, choosing that direction to investigate first.

"Spread out but no further than ten to twelve feet." Matt instructed. He had supplied them with the full-face communication masks enabling them to talk with one another during the search.

"Aye, aye, Mein Capitan!" Kim replied.

"Shut-up," Patti shot back. "Mind your manners."

"On second thought, hang close." Matt said.

"Not much visibility." Patti could barely see three feet in front of her. "Too dangerous, we can't even see each other at 10 feet."

"I know. Let's move more to the center where it's deeper. Maybe that'll help."

"It's a little better," Kim said, the group having reached the river center and able to spread apart. "I think I can see about ten feet all directions. I can see you, anyway." He waved at Matt who didn't respond. "Just trying to be a little friendly."

"I got the message, but stop wasting your oxygen," Matt scolded.

For a while they moved in silence, seeing nothing unusual. When Matt indicated they swim to the opposite shore, they followed, always scanning the perimeters of vision, spear guns held tight. The closer they came to the shore, the murkier the water.

"Nothing here," Matt said. "Let's head downriver."

Swimming back to mid-river and fifteen minutes into the down-river excursion, their oxygen levels had reached a point at which they would need to return to home base. Matt led the way, flanked on his left by Kim, with Patti on the right, but lagging slightly behind the other divers. She continuously scanned the areas through which they swam, keeping the fins of the others in view; but as her visibility became more and more clouded, her intuition signaled that there was a change in the murkiness. Instead of the buoyant brown mud particles that intermingled with the natural dark green of the water, the murk came in clouds, blindingly thick and dark. She turned to look behind but was faced with a brown wall that totally engulfed her body. Her hackles rose and her flesh crawled within the body-suit. *Thump...thump...thump...*it was the beating of her heart. *Something is wrong.* Her sense of direction was lost; it vanished when she had spun to check the encroaching mass. Perhaps in the murkiness the creature couldn't see her, but surely it could pinpoint her exact position by the thumps of her heart alone resonating through the water. If she could hear her heart, could *it?* She stretched her body vertically to feel the depth of her position—and froze. Her fins struck an object, and it was *not* the river bottom; this object moved! She ran her fins over the peaks and valleys of the object; Over one spike, her fins rolled....then another...and *another. My God, it's beneath me!*

Desperate and shaking, her fingers gripped tightly around the spear gun. It was equipped with a power head[i] but the whole apparatus was cumbersome in this time of panic. Her body shook in fear as she pulled her left hand–the one with the wrist compass– within view of her mask. She needed to head northeast sixty degrees–the direction of home base—and fast! She followed its direction, all the while praying that she did not have the same fate as Ted, and Jack, the diver. It took all the self-control she could muster to propel herself forward. Lost were the fins of her companions, she could no longer see them in the distance. *They don't know I'm gone!* If they were unaware that she had lagged too far behind, then they could be of no help!

The clouds of muck continued to rise, sometimes even blocking her view of the compass. Terrified, she resisted the natural urge to look below, to face the stalking creature as it moved beneath her. *Why does it wait?* The sheer anxiety of waiting for it to strike did not calm the thumping of her heart, yet the creature continued its trek along the river bottom, kicking up muck that mushroomed into choking walls of darkness and blinding her to the extent that she could not take aim with the gun.

"Matt! Help!" she screamed into the face mask, glad that she was able to communicate to the others. Had she worn her own equipment she would have faced a far worse ordeal in this situation. "Matt, it's beneath me!"

"Shit," she heard Kim reply.

"We can't see you—where are you?" Matt asked. He could not disguise the panic in his voice.

"I was behind you," she replied, the panic of the situation getting harder to control with every stroke of a fin. "But I…I fell behind. I'm headed to… home base. The thing is…right below me." She gave them her bearing, but in her panic, she had nearly depleted her oxygen supply. Her words were choppy and raspy, as if she had run a great distance to answer a phone call.

"Try not to panic or you'll use up your air! I'm coming back your way."

"Me too," Kim said. "Weapons ready!"

She prayed she would soon see her friends, or at least the upward slope of the river bottom, but before she would finish the thought, she felt the rounded spikes of the carapace strike her belly. Once…twice…and then she was on all fours, her knees resting in the valleys between the osteoderms of the creature's hard and slimy shell. Her head was out of the water…now her shoulders. The creature was smart; the loss of buoyancy worked against her, it kept her pinned onto the creature's carapace. Her compass wrist stretched only partway around a thick and rock-hard osteoderm. The oxygen tank weighed heavy on her back, while the spear gun that she had white-knuckled in one hand, clanked with dull thuds against the carapace. She and the creature moved swiftly, but to where? She had ridden a dolphin once, and was shocked that the speed of this giant anomaly—this freak of nature—that now attempted to steal her away.

She struggled to get a bearing or landmark, and spotted the clearing, the home base, about 200 feet away. This was her only avenue of escape—this very moment. She crawled backward, maneuvering blindly though the osteoderms until the carapace sloped downward toward the tail. She let go, hoping the thick tail would not touch her, alerting the creature of her escape. She did not wait to see what the giant would do when it realized she was gone, she swam like the devil until she felt the river bottom rise to a few short feet beneath her. In a panic she crawled—scrambled—up the slope toward the blessed land, stopping only to remove the full face mask and the heavy vest and tank, leaving them in the shallow waters of the bank. Sobbing, she rose and ran awkwardly, bringing her fins high into the air so as to not trip herself in the escape. When she finally stopped, gasping for air, she turned to look out at the river; the creature had submerged.

After removing her fins, she paced the river bank anxiously waiting for Matt and Kim to return. Did the creature have them? The thumping of her heart had not stopped, it now pounded in fear for them. Their oxygen had been low before they had turned back for her rescue, and she prayed they were safe and would return shortly.

The sight of Buzz Abbot's skiff approaching from behind the thick riverside vegetation startled her. He stopped the motor and stared, as he usually did in her presence. "Ma'am," he said. "Everything okay?"

"You shouldn't be here. It's not safe in the river."

"Not safe?" Buzz raised the boat's motor as he approached the shore. The skiff beached itself on the muddy bottom, and he stepped out into the shallow water.

Now what? Could this day get worse? She took a few steps backward as he approached, trying her best to look nonchalant.

"What's the problem?" he asked, the piercing blue eyes holding her captive.

"I'm waiting for two divers. They'll be here any minute." *I hope.*

"Why isn't the river safe?"

"Listen, Mr. Abbot, there's something out there – something huge and we think it's killing people."

Buzz Abbot scanned the river. "Killing people? What do you think it is?"

"We're not sure. Maybe a big gator." She didn't want to say "turtle".

"Is your man still missing?"

"He is."

"I'm sorry to hear that."

He stood close, *much too close*. His peppered, marine haircut stood out shockingly against his tanned, rugged face. She felt small next to his muscular, broad shouldered torso, and vulnerable. He raised the black flag of warning, and she was on edge.

"I trust that you will keep this information in your confidence. The sheriff is putting 'no swimming' signs up and down the river. We don't want to alarm the public, but we need to keep them safe; we want them out of the water until we remove the...the gator."

Buzz kept his icy blue eyes glued to hers as she spoke. An uncomfortable silence followed in which she shuffled in place, tempted to step away, but held fast. *I can't let him intimidate me. I wish to hell they'd return.*

"Maybe it's a good sign that gators are comin' back— of course not to kill people."

"Of course." She scanned the river for signs of Matt and Kim hoping Buzz Abbot would get the hint that their conversation was over.

"No worries about me telling anyone. I don't see many people." He turned away, following her gaze. "'cept those nosey land developers now and again," he said, nearly inaudibly. "Might be good to tell them, though; make 'em change their minds...."

"There they are!" Patti put a visor-like hand over her brow. "They're coming!" Her elation was evident to Buzz.

"Guess I'll be shoving off then," he said. "Good day to you." He squished through the sludge to his waiting skiff and pushed it further into the water before hopping aboard.

"Good day to you, too." Patti answered, very relieved that he was finally leaving.

* * *

"Thank God you're here!" Kim said, standing waist high in the river removing his equipment.

"Ditto that," Matt said removing his mask. "We searched and searched until we were dangerously low on oxygen." He removed his tank, set it on the ground and unzipped his wetsuit. "Last we heard, the beast was beneath you. Why didn't you tell us you'd reached shore?"

"I'm sorry. I had no time to tell you. I *rode* that creatures back—I was actually on top of the thing! Look, I'm still shaking—and a visit by Buzz Abbot didn't help. That man sends shivers up my spine."

As the trio stood alongside the river, Patti relayed, in depth, her terrifying near-death experience with the immense beast. "This thing is smart; it's a predator in the worst sense. What the heck are we going to do? We can't let it be known that there's a giant man-eating turtle in the river, and we can't let people swim, or even boat for that matter."

"Did you tell Buzz Abbot he couldn't boat?"

"Of course not, and I doubt he'd listen to me in the first place. I told him we thought there was a large gator in the river and to please keep his mouth shut so as not to frighten people. Hopefully he'll pay heed to that warning."

"Who is that guy, anyway?" Kim asked.

"He's a recluse. He's been in the woods from birth, and he gives me the creeps the way he always shows up. What the heck is he doing on the river all the time anyway? There aren't any fish, so he's not fishing."

"And the mystery continues…." Kim wiggled his eyebrows.

As they turned to leave, they didn't see the peaks of the cara-pace rise above the water line in the distance, nor the dark hooded eyes watching their departure.

CHAPTER TEN

Buzz leaned his 30-06 rifle against a tall pine. He had been stalking a doe, but when her ears pricked at the sound of voices she ran off, white tail flagging. The voices reached Buzz's ears at the same time.

"Damn." He needed game, and now his chance was gone. He made note of the rifle's location and walked a short distance, following the muffled sounds to the edge of a clearing where he camouflaged himself into the vegetation. It was a man-made clearing as new developments were approaching his property, boxing him in. *Surveyors*. Two men stood talking by their blue pickup. They unloaded surveying equipment from the back, and then each walked in different directions—one coming directly at Buzz.

He quickly retraced his steps, grabbed his rifle, and aimed in the direction from which he had come. He wanted to kill them, kill them all. *Damned progress!* It wasn't progress to him, it was invasion of his territory. He lowered the rifle and headed back to the cabin. *Not good. Not good at all.* He was being surrounded by townhouses and condos. If this kept up, he would be circled by humans, young adults with screaming children, children who would find adventure in the woods— *his* woods. *Not good at all.* He hated them, and the intrusion into his private world.

Sitting over a bowl of leftover rabbit stew, he pondered the future, and it wasn't pleasant. At a bird's eye view, he envisioned the cabin and his precious woods totally encircled by concrete. His home would, eventually, become like a city park in the middle of suburbia, a spot of green amongst the gray. What could he do to prevent this horror? It wasn't the fault of the surveyors, they were just doing their job. It was the fault of the land developer, that's who. *Go to the source.* If there were no land developers, then the concrete jungles wouldn't rise around him. If there were no land developers, then he could live in peace, in solitude, away from prying eyes as he had always done. He needed a plan; and as if a prayer answered by God, it came to him. He had the solution all the time, and it lived beneath his cabin; *Snapper.*

"Buzz! Buzz! Ain't ya gonna feed me, too?" His father's voice pulled him from his thoughts and just when he had a solution! He hated the sound of *that* voice, and he hated caring for the old man. He wished he could put the old man in a home and forget about him.

"Shut your hollering! I'm coming!" He said, slopping a ladle full of stew into a chipped bowl. Seeing a few rabbit chunks intermingled with the potatoes and carrots, he grabbed a fork and ate them. *No sense giving the old man meat he can't eat without teeth.* He set the bowl on a tray along with a glass of water and made his way to his father's bedroom. It was the same room, the same bed, and the same furniture from his childhood and it always brought back memories of his mother and her horrible death.

"Here," he said, plopping the tray down on Elmer's lap. Elmer managed to scooch himself up to a sitting position, which Buzz knew was a difficult task for the old man, being as weak and decrepit as he was; but he didn't care and didn't offer to help. The tray jiggled with the movement, and water spilled from the glass into the stew.

"You ain't no help, boy. You're useless. Killed your mother, and now you're trying to kill me."

"Shut up," Buzz said, and left, slamming the door behind him. The room stank from the old man. Urine, feces, it was ugly, the whole old age scene and no one here to help him. If his mother had lived, she would be taking care of Elmer, not him. If his mother had lived, things would be different. His father would have still loved him and been his friend.

CHAPTER ELEVEN

Her coffee mug held suspended on its way to her lips. Every once in a while, the hard reality of Ted's death struck home and her body paused—froze— as the memory of him flooded her heart. It was obvious that Ted was not returning. There would be no wedding, no reception, no honeymoon. There would be no growing old together, no children, no grandchildren. On one hand, she was grateful that her deep sorrow in losing Ted had been shelved by her preoccupation with the immediate problem of finding a monster killer on the loose. On the other hand, she felt guilty for the diversion of her attentions. *I won't forget you, Ted.*

"You're thinking of him, aren't you?" Kim asked, sipping his coffee. They sat across from each other at Patti's kitchen table.

She shrugged and wiped a tear from her eye. "Yep. Can't help it. I feel guilty, like I've forgotten him in all the stress of finding the creature. It's like I'm glad that we have this search to occupy our time.

"Ted wouldn't want you crying all the time, would he?"

"No, but I'd sure be mad if he forgot me so fast!" She tried to crack a smile.

"Patti, you haven't forgotten him. You're sitting here holding back tears because you haven't forgotten him. We have a dangerous creature on the loose, and I would think he'd be proud of you for trying so hard to avenge his killer."

"Oh, I know." She reached for a tissue box that had found a newly permanent home nestled in between the salt and pepper shakers on the Lazy Susan.

"As for revenge, when we find the beast, we have to capture and preserve it for study," she said.

"That goes without saying, doesn't it?" Kim replied peering over his black framed glasses. "It's an incredible discovery, Nat Geo stuff; 'The return of the Dinosaur!' I can just see the title of that issue!"

"But poor Ted…you can't imagine how badly and guilty I feel about this. How can I actually want to safeguard Ted's killer?"

"You're a scientist, that's why. Science always comes first, it's our job. Well, *was* our job before you threw it all away to live in a tiny Georgia town in the backwoods with your high school sweetheart."

"How can you say such a thing? I loved Ted!"

"Oops, I'm so sorry! Truly I am." He reached across the table to take her hand. "I lost my head. I'm deeply sorry about Ted, but this turtle thing…it really is an incredible discovery; and it's *us*, you and me, two puny, unknown scientists involved in the middle of a fabulous discovery. Can't help it."

"I wish I could look at it that way without feeling guilty."

"We need to figure out a way to capture it before some crazy yahoo comes in with dynamite and machine guns."

"You're right. Get your thinking cap on, smarty."

* * *

"What?" Sheriff Monroe stared at them in disbelief. She and Kim had come to the station with a plan, a plan to save the beast for future study. "This is a killer we're looking for, not a pet for a zoo!" Monroe exclaimed.

"It's an important discovery, Sheriff," Patti said. "We need to find out how this turtle got so big. Is there something in the river water? I think we've resolved the issue of the missing river life, but what if all turtles got to that size? Will other creatures grow this large? It's better to resolve the problem now, and not later."

"Well, if you put it that way, I suppose you do need to study it, but we can't even find the damn thing so how can we capture it, and where will we put it when we do?"

"It will have to be transported to a facility, and since it's our— well, *Patti's*— discovery, we'll want to work with Charleston." Kim interjected. "First, though, we have to get good photos of the creature or else nobody on earth is going to believe it. Once we do, we'll call in the cavalry."

"Okay, so we know where it's going, and not soon enough as far as I'm concerned. Now, the big question: how do we catch it?"

"Kim and I are still working on that one, Sheriff. First, we have to find out where it's holed up—*if* it's still here. There haven't been any reported missing persons that we should know about, have there?"

"Nope. Do you think it moved on?" Monroe asked.

"I don't know, but it will kill wherever it goes. Due to its size, it will have to feed almost constantly. There's nothing left in the river for it and that leaves what? *Us*, that's what. We have to capture it." Patti said.

* * *

Patti, Kim and Matt hooked their fins in their elbows as they walked into the river under the weight of their tanks. Once chest high, they slipped their feet into the fins, checked their equipment and waved to Sheriff Monroe before submerging. Sheriff Monroe waved and leaned against the hood of his patrol car. The divers submerged and were out of view.

It had been decided by an emergency meeting with the Sheriff and the dive team, which now consisted of Patti, Kim and Matt, that exploration of the river would continue at the first opportunity, which translated to when the weather was calm, as well as the river current. Though the water was still slightly murky from the storm, no time was wasted by the trio. They decided to go ahead with the search, and the very next day they met riverside. Patti was still very nervous considering her past encounter with the creature, but tried very hard to stifle her fears, afraid that Matt would kick her off the team.

"Stick together," Matted reminded them as they submerged. "Upriver first, as planned." Matt carried a spear gun with power head attached, just in case it became necessary.

After 30 minutes of literally seeing nothing suspicious in view, Matt motioned to surface. They tread water in an attempt to catch a clearer view of their surroundings.

"Look over there," Kim said. Isn't that the weird guy you were talking about? What do you suppose he's doing?"

The trio watched silently, their heads bobbing on the surface mid-river. Buzz appeared to be studying the riverbank upon which he stood. He paced, bent to look at the ground, and then paced again, sometimes rubbing the stubble of whiskers that were often seen on his face. A few times he walked to the water's edge and peered over the bank.

"What's he looking at?" Patti whispered, knowing how voices bounced across water.

"I can't imagine," Matt whispered in reply.

After a few minutes of treading water, and after watching Buzz stake an area of ground at the river's edge, the trio submerged, deciding to swim to the other side of the river, look for the beast there and then head back to home base to switch tanks.

* * *

"Maybe he was marking a boat ramp?" Matt said, upon their return to home base.

"Who, Buzz?" Sheriff Monroe asked, listening in on the conversation. The divers sat on fold out chairs, resting before they continued the search. "He already has a boat ramp. Don't know why he would need another one. In fact, the river is deeper at that end, and he built himself a whole dock years ago. He has that skiff, you know."

"And just what does he do out there on the river? I always see him, but there are no fish to catch, thanks to the beast. There's something curious about him," Patti said.

"That ain't new," Monroe laughed. "He and his old man got mighty strange after Jane disappeared. Nothin' was ever the same after that, so we just kinda left them alone."

"And nobody knows what happened to Jane?"

"Nope. I remember how my daddy—he was a sheriff too, you know; family tradition. He took some men and even searched the cabin and area, but never found nothin'."

"Strange man," Patti said under her breath.

The rest of the day turned up nothing. Defeated and tired, the divers gave up the search until the next day. Matt left for home, the sheriff long departed, and Patti and Kim headed to the diner for a quick meal.

"You know what?" Patti asked between bites of a hamburger. "I don't trust that Buzz Abbot. There's something mighty strange about him. I think we should go back to where we saw him today, and if he isn't there tomorrow, let's get closer and see if we can figure out what he was doing."

"I don't know what this has to do with catching the monster," Kim replied, stuffing a French fry into his mouth.

"I don't either, but something bugs me about that man. I want to get a better look."

"Do you honestly think Matt is going to waste time, effort and oxygen examining what a backwoods local was doing by the river today? He could have been doing anything; setting traps, or measuring for a ramp, like you said, or just...just...building a tent platform. How about that idea?

"Why the heck would be build a tent platform, when I'm sure he has a nice comfy bed at home?"

"Just a thought off the top of my head." Kim looked out the picture window next to the booth. "If that's the case, it's still light out. Why don't we go when we're finished here and take a look?"

"Uh, I don't know. I'm not sure where we could park, and we'd have to walk through the woods anyway, to get to the river."

"I don't suppose you know his property line."

"No, but wait...there is another boat ramp entrance to the river near where I think is Buzz's line. We could park there and then make our way through the woods to where we saw him."

"This is crazy, but my idea, though, so let's do it."

* * *

"Well get a load of that. How could I not know this was happening?" Patti was baffled. Upon arriving at their target, they came upon a huge cleared area. Two bulldozers sat parked surrounded by piles of dirt that sat like brown mountains at the edge of the clearing. A large sign set in the ground read "Richard Bandoff Construction."

"Oh my God," Patti whispered. "Now I remember Buzz mumbling something about land developers. I didn't think anything of it, but this must be what he meant. I'm sure he doesn't like this one bit. Can't say I do either."

Kim looked off into the nearby woods. "Do you think that's his land? There are enough 'no trespassing' signs posted."

"Sure is his land. Come on. Let's get out of the car and down to the river."

The trek to the river was tedious considering there was not a path to follow. Branches swiped their arms and legs as they walked over fallen trees, pine cones, pine needles, dropped leaves from the deciduous trees, and through green briar stickers. Twigs and smaller branches crunched beneath their feet. A few squirrels scattered, and birds took flight at their approach, but it was the mosquitos that drove them crazy.

"Of course neither of us thought to bring bug spray...did you...maybe?" Kim asked, continuously slapping his body at the offensive, stinging creatures. "I must be a mosquito magnet."

"Obviously we don't have bug spray, and I don't have a flashlight, either, so let's hurry. I don't want to be stuck out here bitten to death in the dark."

Breaking through the woods to the river, they tread gingerly along its bank toward the site where they had seen Buzz that afternoon. The river was definitely deeper here, as there was not a gentle slope to the deeper water, but a shear drop off. As they had not swam closer to shore after spotting Buzz earlier, they did not know the depth of the water at this point.

"There it is," Patti whispered. "And look! What in the world?"

Seeing that Buzz was not near, they approached the site where he had stood. Steel pipes in two sizes lined up aside the staked area, along with four couplings, bags of cement, and a few pails.

"There's obviously a project going on here, but what? And look at the stakes, they're so far apart. Any guesses?"

"Not a one," Kim replied. He was obviously as perplexed as she. "How far apart do you think those stakes are?"

Patti walked the course from stake to stake. "I'm guessing about sixteen feet. How many pipes are there?"

Kim was already counting. "Three long, and three shorter."

"I'm clueless," she admitted.

"That makes two of us."

"Wait...what's that?" She pointed a distance away into the woods. "There's something blue in there, see it?"

"The mystery continues...."

Once at the site of the object, they stood evaluating this new discovery.

"A tractor with a posthole digger. Interesting," Kim said. "I repeat...the mystery continues...."

"Come on, let's head back before it's too dark to see. We don't want to spend the night in the woods.

CHAPTER TWELVE

"Today we're going to start upriver," Matt informed the group when they met the following day at home base. "I checked out the map and we can start at the next DNR ramp area up the road, and search down from there. The sheriff will meet us at home base at lunchtime."

"Monroe says he can't keep this under wraps much longer since there's a danger to the public," Matt said. "If the beast isn't here, then it's somewhere else, and that means the public has to be warned," Matt said.

"We're just afraid someone is going to come in with heavy arms and blow the thing to kingdom come," Patti said. "We need to study this creature and find out how and why it got so large. This could possibly happen again to other river life, and we have to stop the process, whatever it is."

"I realize that, Patti, and so does Monroe; but you must agree that the public needs to know."

"We need a lead, *today*." Kim said. "There's not enough police force in this town to provide surveillance up and down the whole darn river if a bunch of trophy hunters come in."

"Matt," Patti said, then hesitated. "Uh, Kim and I did some investigating on our own last night. We hiked to the spot where we saw Buzz Abbot yesterday and checked out the stakes by the riverbank. They're about sixteen feet apart. There are long steel pipes there, too, and bags of cement. Not only that, there's a tractor with a posthole digger further back in the woods. He obviously has a project going, but what? What do you suppose he could be doing?"

"That is kind of strange," Matt replied after a moment of thought. "But it's not our concern. Our concern is locating this creature, and soon."

"Do you think that when we pass that spot we can get a little closer to the shore?" Patti asked. "The water is deep there, judging by the drop off into the river, but I don't know how deep. It would only take a moment."

Matt thought a moment before answering. "Well...I suppose so, but only if our air supply is sufficient by that time."

At the river's access, suited and submerged, they began their dive. The river was calm, and the water, though murky green, still provided enough visibility to see ahead ten to fifteen dense feet. Patti had put to memory the approximate distance to Buzz's land as they had driven past the thickly overgrown entrance to his cabin. Now, as they swam and investigated mid-river, she kept pace on her GPS knowing that if they passed it by, Matt would not return to the spot. As was the case throughout the area, the water was void of life except for the small minnows that were now in abundance, considering there was nothing to eat them, nothing to equalize the environmental balance of nature. At times it was as though they swam through millions of the small fish, fish that could not possibly satisfy the hunger of the ravenous beast for which they searched.

Patti viewed her wrist GPS and stopped. "It's around here," she said into the mask, and the others stopped. Matt inserted a way point on his GPS. "Surface," he said.

Patti tried to clear off the front of her mask, but it was futile. "I don't think he's there, but it's hard to tell with the mask on." She wanted to approach above the water in case she caught sight of Buzz and could warn the others, but with an unclear visual she joined the others who had re-submerged.

The water was surprisingly deep, and when the bank became visible to the divers, they stopped. "Look at that dark spot," she said, pointing to a large black area partially obscured by overhanging brush from above.

As the divers swam closer, Patti was first to reach the dark patch. "Oh, my God. It's a cave, and it's huge!" She knew there were smaller underwater crevices in the area—crevices where the locals went noodling for catfish—but a cave! The entrance began approximately three to four feet below the surface, and perhaps more than a dozen feet or so in depth. A strong current flowed from the entrance out into the larger river

"Wow," Kim said. "An underground river! Shall we?"

"It's worth a shot," Matt said. "Let's take a look."

One by one, they entered the cave, turning on their headlamps, as the sun no longer filtered here. Around twenty-five feet into the cave, which was as wide as it was high, they approached a split; one forked off to the right into a narrow passage, while the other appeared to be a continuation of the main tunnel.

Matt stopped. "Let's head to home base and come up with a plan. I think we've hit the jackpot. "

As they headed back to the entrance, the current changed. It became stronger, with a powerful "whoosh" that sent them forward a few feet as if they were riding a wave.

"Is it coming?" Patti' eyes shone large through her mask as she questioned Matt. They rapidly continued their swim to the entrance and immediately hugged the bank, clutching at roots, overhanging vegetation and whatever else they could find to keep themselves still.

"Oh shit," Kim said, as he had separated from the trio and was on the opposite side of the opening. "I'm alone!"

"Quiet!" Matt whispered, and just in time, as a cloud of muck shot out of the cave, along with the most terrifying sight of river life scientist or diver had ever witnessed. The shocking vision stunned them into absolute silence. Breath, which had come in a steady rise and fall echoing in the divers' ears through their regulators, was now stilled and silent as death.

Behind the blast of muck came the beast. Through the clouded mixture of brownish water and river bottom, a hideous head emerged. Patti's eyes widened in terror, and her body trembled as the beast passed. *As big as a house!* It propelled itself beyond the stilled divers with dangerously clawed forefeet, its peaked carapace streamed with ribbons of algae. When it turned to swim downriver—and blessedly not sensing the intruders— they saw the lengthy, sharpened points of its beak open with jaws that appeared as wide as the cavern entrance itself, and watched in disbelief as it headed downstream engulfing a school of minnows who unknowingly had entered a cavern of death.

"My God," Matt whispered. "It's headed toward home base. Monroe will be there by now."

Patti clawed frantically at the roots of the bank looking for an escape route. *I have to get out of here!* Fear had overtaken any shred of sensibility she had left in her head. Her entire body now trembled uncontrollably. Her large diver fins flopped ineffectively against the craggy wall of the river as she searched for a foothold.

"You're panicking." Matt held her now, his hands on her hips in an attempt to stop her frantic actions. "Calm down!"

By the time they found enough leverage to climb out of the water—and much too near Buzz's project—Patti was sobbing, hysterically. "Oh my God, did you see it? Did you see it?"

"We saw it," Matt answered.

"We did," Kim echoed. "And I feel just like you, only my masculine pride won't let me freak out. I may have raised the water level a tad...."

Patti managed a slight smile. "I'm sorry," she said wiping her eyes with the palm of a hand. "I lost control. I know better, but....oh my God to think that this is how Ted died, by that—that thing! It's horrid. How did it get that way?"

"Listen," Matt said, sitting next to her on the riverbank. "That *thing* is headed down river, and Sheriff Monroe is downriver waiting for us. We need to get back there, and quick."

"Not to mention that we're on the weird one's property." Kim interjected.

"I...I'm afraid to get back in the river, Matt. This is awful. It's never happened to me before that I could be so frightened of something."

"Remember that hungry Maco shark we ran into once?" Kim asked. "This is worse th..."

Matt shot him a dirty look.

"This *is* worse, I can't stop shaking," Patti agreed.

At that moment, all heads turned toward Buzz's project at the snap of a twig, the sound of someone approaching through the woods.

"Is he coming?" she whispered.

"Could be. Come on, let's go." Matt slid off the bank into the water, followed by Kim.

"Come on," Kim said. We're between a rock and a hard place; get in here."

Patti looked in the direction of the ground stakes. A flash of white came into view between the trees—just enough to send her slipping into the water. She repositioned her mask and checked her air gauge; it was going fast. "Will we make it? My oxygen is low."

"Ours too. Let's get as far down as we can. Can't be too much longer, and don't talk unless necessary."

Aside from their shattered nerves, the swim toward home base was uneventful. Patti's heart drummed—pounded— in her ears as she swam, and she constantly craned her neck searching for the return of the beast; but it did not appear to be in the area. When their oxygen became too low to continue, the trio headed for shore. The water was much shallower at this section, and they were able to walk up a gentle slope. Matt removed his mask, headlamp and tank as he splashed his departure from the river. "We'll have to walk the rest of the way. Leave the tanks in the brush, and we'll get them later."

"I can swim the rest of the way, thank you. I'll stick close to shore," Kim said.

"You'll do no such thing," Matt replied. "We stick together; it isn't safe in there."

"I can't believe you'd even consider going alone." Patti scolded, holding her fins and gingerly following Matt as he broke through brush into the woods. Any chance of walking the shoreline for the next twenty to thirty feet was impossible, as the lush landscape crept thickly to the river's edge.

They arrived at home base quite bedraggled, scratched and bitten, and looking forward to disposing of their suits and fins, when Matt stopped them cold, holding out his arm to keep them from progressing further. "I was afraid of this," he said.

"What? I can't see!" Kim stretched his neck to peek around Matt's bulky frame.

"Oh my God!" Patti felt a bolt of terror strike like lightning. "The sheriff!"

Kim scooted around the two and then scooted back rapidly when he caught sight of the total destruction of the base. "It's been here! Where's Sheriff Monroe?"

"Sheriff!" Matt called, and stepped down to the river, bypassing the overturned and crushed Sheriff's vehicle, the diving equipment scattered haphazardly about, and...a hand, a bloody ragged hand that still held a gun.

"My God!" Patti screamed, her eyes settling on the bloody remains. "Matt, maybe he's hurt in the woods; we have to find him!"

Matt sat on the fallen log where Ted had set his clothes on the last day of his life, and despairingly placed his head in his hands. "This is a nightmare. It's bigger than we can handle, and we have to call it in...we need help."

"Our phones are in the dive van, remember?" Kim said, still standing at the edge of the woods.

"Start looking for Monroe and his phone," Patti ordered, setting out for the lower brush that edged the home base. As she and Kim searched, Matt studied the overturned, crushed vehicle. "There should be a radio in here." He got on all fours and tried to squeeze into the driver's side. "Any luck with the phone?" he yelled, grunting as he snaked the upper part of his body through the narrow opening, always mindful of the glass shards that hung like shark's teeth from the window's edge.

"Not yet," came the reply.

"Keep looking. I can't see a damn thing in here at this angle. The wetsuit isn't helping mobility."

Patti put a tight eye on the river, watching for the beast to return. After scanning the waters up and down, and satisfied that the creature was gone, she returned to the phone search. "Poor Monroe" she said under her breath. "Poor Ted." She couldn't–and didn't–want to dwell on the horror that the creature's victims had suffered.

Several minutes passed before a static sound came from the sheriff's car. "You got it!" Patti yelled.

"Not quite," was the muffled reply. "I got it but can't see what the heck I'm doing, not to mention everything is topsy-turvy in here. It's too much to ask for a flashlight, right?"

Patti and Kim looked at one another and shrugged. "Just the headlamps we wore. Shall I get yours? It's right here. Everything else is in the van," she said, bending over Matt's now prone body. Maybe I should walk back to the access?"

"We'll all go together. Just hold on a second while I get out of here."

Busy with the radio, no one registered the sound of a disturbance at the river's surface.

"Whew, smell that? What the heck?" Kim asked, sniffing the air.

"Do you need a hand?" Patti ignored Kim's comment and outstretched her arm to help Matt as he emerged from the shattered window.

"Sure smells like low tide," Kim said, turning toward the river. "Oh...my... God!" he said, beneath his breath. "It's here!"

"Get up Matt, and fast." Patti said quietly, fighting back the impulse to panic and run. "*It's back.*" Her voice was low and steady, but not without constraint; she wanted to scream. The beast was still, its beady eyes staring, its outtake of breath creating bubbles on the water. Its mottled carapace peaked far above the surface, as the river was shallow at the point at which it had settled.

Patti and Kim pulled Matt to his feet, and they slowly backed off toward the woods, keeping their eyes on its unwavering stare.

"It's watching us. Shhh, no quick moves!" Patti warned.

"Don't worry, I don't plan on being his next meal," Kim said backing further into the brush.

"I don't think he can get through the trees."

"Me neither, Matt. Keep going."

Suddenly, the beast opened its jaws sending out a guttural hiss of foul air strong enough to wave the tall grasses that preceded the woods.

"It's coming!" Kim said, and they watched in rising horror as it began its ascent to shore. Slowly, as if there was nothing in the world to hurry for, it lifted one giant clawed foot after another out of the river until it stood in revolting splendor on the river bank, its great beak chomping at air, as its overpowering stench permeated the atmosphere of the clearing.

Snap, snap, snap went the sharpened points of its killer jaws as it swung its massive head from side to side. With each nightmarish swing, it stepped forward, a guttural hiss resonating from deep within its body.

"Incredible!" Patti whispered.

"I'm getting out of here," Kim replied, and turned to smash his way through the brush. The others followed, reaching the safety of the trees. They turned to see that the creature, realizing its prey was escaping, clamored forth on legs as wide as Roman pillars—legs as bitterly ugly to the eye as was the rest of its mutant body. The overturned car crunched even more as the beast straddled the wreck, the metal of the car's underside scraping in agonizing decibels against the bottom of the beast's carapace. It was coming fast now, a direct line of attack—until it reached the trees.

The dirt road of escape fell to the left but they didn't dare exit in full view of the creature, not knowing how fast it could run—or even *if* it could run—so they turned away and continued deeper into the woods. Sooner or later they would come to the access road and, hopefully, safety. Looking behind, the trees blocked their vision and the creature could only be seen in cuts and pieces viewed through the tall pines and deciduous trees. It appeared to be pacing, but breaking through the woods did not seem an easy task for the beast. When they turned to look again, it was gone, or obscured by the thickening forest.

"Maybe it went back to the river. Do you think?" Kim asked.

"God, I hope so," Patti said. There was so much to think about, so many unanswered questions regarding this new and mutated species; how far could it see? Did it have a sense of smell? Where did it come from? How did he get that way? Hopefully, the creature would return to its tunnel and let them get to work. They needed time, and lots of it.

CHAPTER THIRTEEN

The monster in the river was no longer a secret. Something had happened, and it wasn't good. Divers flooded the river like schools of fish. Buzz watched from his skiff, camouflaged in the overhang of tree limbs and Spanish moss. Deputy Dave stood on shore along with Patti, who nervously paced the small landing. Buzz wondered why she wasn't diving. He had witnessed at least five or six divers enter the river in the short time he was there, but not her. He decided the only way to find out the whole story was to approach the two on shore and ask.

* * *

"Oh, no," Patti whispered, having caught sight of Buzz puttering toward them in his skiff. "Look who's coming, Dave." Where were the others when she needed them? Matt was out in the river with the other rescue divers, and Kim was investigating another missing person report about 50 miles upriver. *At least Dave is here!*

Buzz approached as far as he could before stepping out of the skiff into knee-deep water. "Good day," he said, nodding to both Patti and Deputy Dave, then walked the few steps to the bank and tied his bow line to the fallen log.

"Hello, Buzz. Hot day, huh?" Dave greeted.

"I see there are lots of divers up and down the river. That big gator still out there? Can you fill me in?"

"You know Sheriff Monroe was killed, don't you?" Dave asked.

Patti noted the look of shock on Buzz's face. "The sheriff was killed—*taken* is a better word—right here where we're standing. I'm surprised you haven't heard about it."

"No…that's awful. I…I've been away for a couple days. What happened? Do you know?"

"Yes, I do know. There's a monster in the river, a giant Alligator Snapping Turtle, and it's killing people," Patti said.

Buzz looked blank for a moment, then his eyebrows furrowed and his eyes hardened as he peered at them in silence. "That's pretty impossible, wouldn't you say?"

"Under normal circumstances I would say it's impossible, but I've seen it with my own eyes," Patti replied.

He looked across the water. "Not good," he whispered beneath his breath, but she heard him.

"No, it's not good. You shouldn't be out there boating."

"You two shouldn't be standing here, in that case." He turned his icy stare to her.

"Well, hell, I'm workin', Buzz," Dave said, and stepped away from the pair apparently to live up to his proclamation.

"The divers are out there now, as you've noticed. I'm waiting for them to return to change tanks, then I hope to go in."

"Are any other people missing, besides Ted and that other….?

Other? Other diver? How would he know? "A young couple disappeared a while back; they were camping on the river down toward Savannah. Then Ted, then *another* diver…" she paused to see if there was a reaction, but he stood staring pensively at her through his pale, squinted eyes. "The diver was killed shortly after Ted disappeared, and now Sheriff Monroe is dead. I've seen this monster, and it has to be stopped."

"You've seen it?"

"Yes, and it's terrifying."

"How many divers are out there now?" he asked.

"Six at the moment."

Buzz scowled. "Guess I'd better get off the river as you say."

"I think you'd better." *Those eyes, the way he stares.* She was relieved that he was leaving and watched as he untied the rope from the log and wordlessly pushed off.

Why didn't he ask what the creature looks like, or ask how big it is? She took her cell phone out of a pocket and called Kim. "Listen, she said. "Creepy Buzz was just here, and I can't shake the feeling that he has something to do with this. We'll look into that later, but for now, while you're checking out that missing person report, start checking parks and whatever alongside the river as far north as you can go. Check its tributaries too; the Tugaloo, the Chattooga and the Seneca. I have a hunch there are more people missing than we know.

CHAPTER FOURTEEN

B uzz docked the skiff and literally ran to his cabin. He opened the trap door, grabbed a flashlight and entered the stairway to the cave. Shining the light ahead, he walked the dark, damp narrowing path of the cavern's river. Soon, the path ran out and the water reached his ankles. "Come on, you beast," he whispered. Terror crept up his spine as he walked; it always did when he feared Snapper was near. The putrid odor of the beast would signal his presence, but he was obviously absent. Buzz didn't smell him this time and thought perhaps he was still in the river. "Damn," he muttered. He wanted to trap Snapper as soon as possible. Otherwise, the cops would be snooping around and ruin his plans. He turned to head back to the cabin. It was just as well that Snapper wasn't present, as he had traveled too far in the tunnel and might have had trouble escaping in time, had he come face to face with the beast.

Neither he, nor his father, ever learned exactly how far back the tunnel ran before it entered into the big river, they only knew that it became deeper and deeper, disappearing into the flow. As he walked back to the stairway, his thoughts drifted to the pain Snapper had caused in his lifetime; to his father, who so mercilessly accused him of letting his mother die. He thought of his mother and her horrible death, and his father's withdrawal of love for his son. His father hated him, and he hated his father.

As he approached the high cavern that led to the Great Way, he stopped, his hackles rose. He sniffed the cool, humid air and inhaled Snapper's putrid odor. He aimed the flashlight down the dark passage from which he had come, one foot ready to run. When at last the light bounced off the beast's head, Snapper's trunk-like legs splashed in rapid succession through the shallows, a giant nightmare coming closer by the second—too close for comfort. Buzz quickly ran through the Great Way and then the curved passage, stopping behind the steel bars that kept Snapper at bay. He flashed the light toward the sound of hisses, thuds and scraping claws that quickly approached. *Sonofabitch is after me!* Then, the beast materialized around the curve of the wall, stopping to eye his foe, his putrid breath sending blasts of foul air that permeated the dead end of the safe spot. Buzz gagged and coughed. "Gotcha, bastard!"

* * *

"Now's the time," he said, setting the lantern on the kitchen table. He opened the refrigerator and removed two dead chickens, feathers and all, wrapped in plastic. He grimaced and gagged; they smelled nearly as bad as Snapper's breath. Again he entered the cavern hoping that Snapper had remained within view, and he had.

"Here, you curse of nature!" Buzz yelled, removing the plastic bags and throwing the carcasses beyond the steel bars.

Snapper hissed at the sound of his voice, and approached. The chickens disappeared in a flash, eaten whole, one by one. He then approached the bars, lowering his beastly head to stare into Buzz's eyes.

Buzz remained, staring back. They had played this game before, *the staring game.* He often wondered if Snapper was remembering the family that had raised him when they shared these moments, or perhaps he was sizing up his next meal. Whatever the reason, it was a moment of truce; neither was trying to kill the other.

"Go away, Snapper." Buzz said quietly after a few moments, and turned to climb the stairway. In the kitchen he closed the trap door and headed to the project—the project that had taxed his endurance to the limit.

The past week he had set to work furiously by the river. Mosquitos buzzed and bit as he dug, drilled, and poured cement. He only worked when the construction crew was not working, so as not to alert them to any activities in the woods—*his* woods. *How dare they,* he thought. *How dare they bring their machines to my land?* He sometimes wished he could borrow the work crew, as the project would go so much quicker, but of course that was impossible. He persevered, though, working throughout the night, or in daylight, squeezing in the time when he didn't see the worker's trucks pull up, or that full-of-himself big shot builder, Richard Bandoff himself, strutting around the site like a rooster. He would teach him, just wait and see.

The project stood approximately eighteen feet in height from the bottom of the river and sixteen feet in width, enough to cover the opening of the cavern entrance beneath, in the bowels of the river. The steel bars were a bitch to work with, and as a lone person creating the construction, he wasn't sure it would even hold. Starting behind the tree line to obscure the project from any passing boats, he dug holes four feet apart in a horizontal line until he hit solid rock—rock of which he didn't know the thickness. First though, it was required of him to verify that the poles would cover the cavern opening once they were inserted, and that required entering the river and swimming into the cavern opening itself to check the width. This he could only do when he knew for certain that Snapper had left. But, he never knew for certain; so he had ventured into the cave a few feet only, holding his breath and keeping a watchful eye for the beast at all times. Once measured, he could only guess the width of the cavern opening from atop the land, but figured he couldn't be far off in his estimation.

With the tractor outfitted with a posthole digger, he slaved through three nights drilling through the hard rock until he struck the river water. At night, when he slept his fitful sleep, the drilling of rock hammered his head until he woke and swung his legs to the floor holding his pounding head in his hands. *It will be worth it*, he thought, battling the horrific headaches. *Once I capture him, it will be worth it.*

Next, he attached the couplings to twelve foot pipes, with eight foot additional piping. To guide the pipes into the drilled holes would be a challenge, so he created rough guides at the holes with cement, just high enough to guide the pipes into place. With each pipe placed, he would drive them into the river bottom with a sledge hammer. The finished project was to be a steel jail from which Snapper could not escape. Three pipes four feet apart would keep the beast trapped. *He hoped.*

Now, with Snapper inside the cavern, he had the chance to set his plan to motion. One by one, Buzz inserted the pipes into the drilled holes with the tractor. It was a bitch of a job, and he cursed Snapper every step of the way for making it necessary. The pipes were heavy, and some caught on the rough cement guides and wouldn't insert into the drilled channels without several tries. It was truly a job for more than one man, but this was *his* project, his alone, and he endured the agonizing and difficult task of inserting the pipes. Sweat poured, mosquitos buzzed and bit, as well as the deer flies, but one by one the poles hit their mark in the cavern entrance below. Once done, and the pipes were pounded into place, he was far too tired to enter the river to inspect his work. *Later,* he thought. *I'll go later.* Wearily, he returned to the cabin and collapsed into a deep sleep.

CHAPTER FIFTEEN

"Now we know what Buzz's project was," Matt said, standing in his wetsuit. "He's trying to keep that beast either inside or out of the cave, but why? He's known all along about that turtle. I sent two divers into the cave. I told them no further than 50 feet. Now, they're missing."

"Man, I've never experienced anything like it!" another diver said. "All of a sudden there was a thud from inside the cave. We thought the beast was coming, but nothing happened, just the thud. Then Don here," he motioned to another diver removing his suit. "He was several feet into the cave and came back out to say that a metal pipe had fallen through from above and damn near impaled him!"

"I surfaced for a look-see," Matt said. It wasn't entirely clear from my end, but through the trees, I saw a tractor working and caught a glance of Buzz driving it. After that, we went in far enough to investigate what was happening, when another pipe fell through!" Matt said. "We told our cave divers to get out—and fast— but they said that the tunnel extended quite a distance and they wanted to go a little further. Then we lost communication."

"A nightmare...," Patti said, wringing her hands. "Buzz was here earlier today. He seemed surprised about Sheriff Monroe, and shocked when I told him about the creature. Then he left, kind of in a hurry now that I think of it."

"We'll be calling in the state troopers, the National Guard and whoever else we need to catch this beast. Too bad we don't have good photos."

Patti dreaded trying to convince anyone that a giant alligator turtle was killing people, and especially since neither she, Matt nor Kim had been able to properly photograph the beast. The only photos were the ones she had taken of the osteoderms after Ted had disappeared. "We definitely need photos," she said, more to herself than to anyone.

"We need a better plan. We're no match for that creature," Matt replied.

"Let's hope our guys make it back in one piece," Don said peeling himself out of the wetsuit.

"I sure hope so, but I'm going back to see if there's any sign of them. I need one more diver."

"I'm coming," Patti started for her dive suit.

"No, you're not."

"What? This is *my* case, if you recall."

"And I'm the dive captain, if you recall."

She had no choice but to obey, and watched begrudgingly from shore as Matt and another diver submerged. It was nerve-racking to wonder what was happening below the surface, and infuriating that she was forbidden to dive.

"This is ridiculous. I'm leaving," she said after a while. She had run out of patience. If Matt wouldn't let her investigate *in* the river, then she would investigate *above* the river. Hopefully Kim had come up with new clues in his research, so she would track him down. "Listen, guys, if that thing surfaces, forget running to your cars. That beast can run cars over like a steam roller. You saw the sheriff's car."

Dave answered by placing a hand on his holstered pistol.

"And that little firearm would be like a pinprick," she added, not knowing why she was taking it all out on the poor fellow. "I'm sorry," she said. I don't mean to be in such foul humor. I'm leaving, so just keep your eyes open and do as I say. If it appears, head deep into the woods. It didn't chase after us when we did the same. It can't break through the trees."

* * *

Patti stared in disbelief at the papers in her hand. "Oh my God," she said, leafing through the seemingly endless list of missing persons. As far back as 1995, in the river and its tributaries, people went missing all the way up to the Carolinas. The young, the old, and in a rare case, an entire family had disappeared mysteriously. "I can't believe that nobody ever put two and two together and figured there was something very mysterious happening."

"I looked into that very question, being the genius I am," Kim said, stroking his gelled and peaked hair, careful not to ruin his do. "There were investigations, but we're dealing with more than one state. A few of the missing turned up dead, murdered, or elsewhere, but I'd say at least half of the missing person cases are unsolved."

"We have a very smart river monster here. It appears he has never been spotted before now."

"Perhaps it took him a long time to get this big?"

"Alligator snappers grow quickly, but…wait…maybe you have something there. What if it stayed a normal size for quite a while and then had a mysterious and abnormal growth spurt?"

"Food for thought," Kim said.

CHAPTER SIXTEEN

*S*napper raised his prehistoric head. The folds of his scaled serpentine neck stretched to nearly the length of his mottled, spiked carapace. He sniffed the dank cave air. Something had awakened him, a splash...then another, and another. Voices vibrated throughout the cavernous passage until the vibrations reached his resting place in the shallow end. In this section of the river, the water was not deep enough to cover his immense body. He lowered his head until it was partially submerged, and from that position he tasted something unusual in the water—unusual in that it normally did not appear in his domain. This particular taste was one that he preferred; it made him hungry.

With the enticing flavor so near, he raised his body onto his sturdy legs to seek his prey. His prey was making sounds, sounds that filled the cavern; sounds that echoed and bounced off the dank walls of his den. The sounds reached his inner ears in dull muffled tones, and again he sniffed the air as his head loped from side to side in an attempt to spot his prey. His vision was sharp but it was pitch black in his den, leaving his sense of smell to do the work.

He lumbered forward in the dark passage toward the river's entrance. A sudden flash of light blinded him for a millisecond, and he blinked. Then there were two bright spots that danced on the ground, the ceiling, and the walls. He was confused, but continued slowly. The lights disappeared, then reappeared as he turned a slight curvature in the passageway. Now both the lights blinded him, and as they did so he heard a tremendous uproar. Though blinded by the bright lights, there was no mistaking the ruckus of the prey's excitement. Suddenly, the lights left his eyes and were now flashing in the opposite direction, the direction of the cavern opening. He heard his prey moving down the passage, splashing and emitting sounds of alarm. Sometimes he could *make out the forms of the prey in the foreground. He knew the prey would be good to eat but possibly difficult to catch, as the prey was not in one piece, but in two.*

He quickened his pace, and as he did so the sounds from the prey became very loud. Sometimes the lights flashed in his eyes again, and he had to stop. The flashes hurt his eyes, and he opened his powerful beak to hiss his dislike. The prey made more sounds when he complained, but the prey didn't stop; the pieces continued to move down the passage following the spots of light.

His luck changed when part of the prey fell. He quickly took advantage of the situation. The other part of the prey didn't move, but pulled on the fallen prey while the blinding light bounced haphazardly against the cavern walls. The light bounced to his eyes again, but it was too late for the prey; he was on it. One heavy foot stomped on the piece that had fallen, while his serpentine neck stretched to pierce the piece that stood with the bright light. The prey wiggled in his jaws and made loud sounds, but soon was silent, as was the piece of prey beneath his razor sharp claws. As he chomped his meal, he spit out pieces of the outside part of the prey. He didn't like the taste of the outside, but the inside was good. Lately, the outside of his prey had a strange coating, but that was the only food he was able to catch because the river was empty of food. Soon, he would have to move on.

CHAPTER SEVENTEEN

Patti pulled her car to a stop beside the Bandoff construction sign. Phone in hand, she exited the car. Kim was certainly not happy about tagging along, now that he knew the truth about Buzz's project.

"Look, there's another car here." He pointed to a Cadillac Seville parked across the field close to the edge of the forest.

"That's odd." Patti raised her phone and snapped a shot of the car. "I wonder who that belongs to, and why would they leave it there in the first place?"

Question unanswered, they proceeded to the edge of the woods, first stopping at the Cadillac for a peek through its windows while they sprayed themselves with bug spray.

"Definitely odd," Kim said. "Kinda gives me the creeps, though; a monster on the loose, a crazy lunatic with his steel pipe trap, and now a mysterious—not to mention expensive—car parked out here in nowheresville. And this is a crazy idea to begin with."

"Maybe so," Patti answered, "but I think we need photos of Buzz's project since we don't have any good ones of the creature. It's a start.

"Why don't we just leave this to the official investigators? We should be talking with Charleston and coming up with a way to preserve the turtle before they jump the gun and blow it to bits."

"Ouch! Darn brambles!" Patti stopped to rub her calf. Indeed the thick woods and brush were a dangerous labyrinth without a trail to guide them. "We'll get right on it after we take the photos," she said. "Promise."

On the riverbank itself, there was nothing to see of the pipes. The flagged markers were gone, as well as the pipes. Kim and Pattie looked at each other and shrugged. "What the heck?" Kim said.

"Matt said there were pipes inserted, but where? Let's check the edge of the woods. Spread out."

After a few minutes, Patti called Kim over to her spot behind the trees. "Look," she said, pointing to the three holes spaced approximately four feet apart.

"Well, what did we expect, a standing jail cell?"

They inspected the three drilled holes, three semi-circular mounds of rough, lumpy cement cupping the far side of each hole, and that was that. Patti proceeded to photograph each in turn, focusing as close as possible to create a clear, detailed photo, while Kim exited the woods to peer over the drop-off into the river. "Maybe we'll see Matt down there," he said, getting on all fours.

"Kim, run!" Patties voice broke through the trees like a thunder clap.

Kim shot to his feet. "What is it? What's wrong? You're scaring the crap out of me!"

"Run!" she screamed again, and then burst through the trees, stumbling to keep her balance. Behind her came Buzz Abbot, rifle in hand.

"Shut up, bitch!" he yelled. "You two get together."

"Wha…?" Kim started to ask, but was rudely silenced.

"You shut up too, chink." Buzz aimed the rifle at him. "Now get together."

Patti stepped to Kim's side at the end of the riverbank drop-off and took hold of his hand; it was trembling, as was her own.

"You just had to snoop, didn't you? Nobody can fucking leave me alone back here on my own land. You've left me no choice."

"No choice?" Patti asked. "No choice about what?"

"Move it." Buzz ordered, pointing his rifle in the direction of a path. "And give me that phone."

Can't! She slowly moved the phone behind her, keeping an eye on Buzz and his rifle. "Can't do, sorry," she said, gratified to hear the phone plop into the water with a silent prayer to Matt. *Please find it!*

Buzz's pale eyes lit like a bonfire. "Bitch!" he yelled. "I ought to shoot you dead right now—the both of you!"

Kim's hand tightened on Patti's. "Wha'd you do that for?" he whispered.

"To save us," she whispered back.

"Shut up!" Buzz stepped forward placing the rifle barrel into Patti's abdomen. "You…just wait." He spat. "I'll take care of you later. Now move!"

For a brief moment it crossed Patti's mind that they could jump into the water. It would be so easy, one step backward. But then they'd be fish in a barrel, and he could shoot them just as easily as if on land.

Buzz waved them forward; and hand in hand, she and Kim took the lead, Buzz's rifle pushing her ahead. "Where are you taking us?" she asked.

"You'll find out soon enough, so just shut up and keep walking."

"Listen," she said. "They're on to you, you know. We're all aware that you knew about this giant beast from day…."

This time the rifle poked her hard enough to make her stumble.

"I told you to shut up!"

"Shut up…," Kim whispered. "We're in trouble enough."

"You too, chink!" Buzz said gruffly.

Soon, they arrived at Buzz's cabin allowing the hostages a brief look around the yard. *Here I am at last,* Patti thought, remembering the dare in high school to peek into the cabin windows in the dark. Rumor had it then that Buzz's mother had come to a questionable end. Taking in the run-down appearance of the general outdoors; rubber tires in a pile, an old truck, a rusted tractor, a collapsing shed taken over by the brambles, a few boarded windows on the cabin, these were just a few things of note that before the screen door squeaked open, then a wooden door, and then entrance into an outdated kitchen.

"You can sit next to my friend there," Buzz said, waving the menacing rifle toward the vinyl covered kitchen table.

Patti's eyes grew large. She looked at Kim, who also appeared to be as shocked as she. At the table sat a thick-set man in dark khaki trousers. He wore an expensive pale yellow sweater accented with several rounds of rope that tied him firmly to a high-backed wooden chair. More to his misfortune, he was gagged and had a seriously blackened eye. The good eye showed unreserved terror, which did nothing to calm Patti's fear as to what was to come.

"Oh, my God. What's going on here?" she asked. "You can't get away with something like this when the whole county—and maybe the whole country by now—knows what a creep you are."

Buzz grabbed Patti by fistful of her cropped hair and pulled her close. "Shut up!" he said through barred teeth, spittle spraying her face.

"Leave her alone!" Kim lunged at Buzz, but Patti was thrown aside against the kitchen sink, and in a flash the rifle went off sending Kim screaming to the floor.

"Oh, my God, what have you've done!" Patti ran to her injured friend and knelt beside him.

"It's my arm!" Kim moaned, blood gushing between his fingers as he held tight to the bullet wound on his upper right arm.

Buzz again grabbed Patti by her hair, yanking her up to a standing position. "Sit next to my friend, there!" he ordered. "You," he motioned to Kim. "You see that trapdoor under the table?"

Kim moaned, turning his head toward the table. Tears ran down his cheeks. "You asshole, you shot me!"

"Answer me, chink! You see that trapdoor under the table?"

"Yes! Yes!" he yelled in reply.

"Open it and get on down there."

"No! I can't move. I'm hurt." He moaned.

Buzz rammed the rifle butt down hard on Kim's abdomen. He screamed in pain, bringing his knees up to his chest. "God, oh God, help me!"

"Stop it!" Patti screamed.

"God Dammit, sit in the chair!" Buzz yelled and pointed the rifle in her direction. "Sit down, or I'll shoot my friend, there." He nodded toward the stranger tied to the chair.

Patti reluctantly replied, her heart breaking for Kim's anguish. The man in the chair was sweating. She noticed bloodstains on the gag.

"Now open the damn door!" Buzz ordered. This time, Kim scooted on his back to the trap door beneath the table. There was no handle, but two finger holes, which he attempted to open with his good arm, but failed; it was too difficult a task with his injury.

"You," Buzz said, pointing the rifle at Patti. Open the door for him."

She glared at Buzz, but reluctantly climbed under the table. With much difficulty, she managed to lift the door. It was heavy, but hinged, so she laid it back until it rested on the floor. "Hang tight, Kim," she whispered.

"I need help," he whispered in return. "This hurts so bad!"

"I didn't say talk, did I?" Buzz stood overhead, his faded jeans all that Patti could see from her position beneath the table.

"Try and stop the bleeding when you get down there. Use your tee shirt and apply pressure." Patti's voice was so low she wondered if Kim could even hear her words.

"Get out of there, now!" Buzz ordered, giving her a kick. She backed out and stood. Buzz motioned again to the chair, and she sat.

"You get down those stairs," Buzz said to Kim.

Kim turned onto his side with much groaning and peered into the opening. "It's dark down there, I can't see."

"Well that's the point, chink. You're trouble, so get down there."

"Oh, my God," he said beneath his breath. It took much maneuvering and cries of pain for him to manage the stairway. He went down on his behind, step by step, with thumps that were heard by all in the kitchen. "I'm down, you bastard!" he yelled, at last. "I'm Asian, not a *chink,* and I'm a hell of a lot smarter than you could ever hope to be."

"Close the door." Buzz ordered. Again, Patti got on all fours and crawled beneath the table.

"I'll get you out of there, Kim. I promise."

"I can't see anything, Patti. It's pitch black!"

"I promise I'll get you out!" she said, tears streaming down her cheeks. She felt so much more vulnerable without Kim nearby; but raising the door, she let it fall shut with a bang. "You're an animal," she said, standing face to face with Buzz.

"And you're asking for pain, girl, aren't you? Is that what you want? You want me beating on you to shut you up? Now sit down with my friend there."

She had no recourse but to sit.

* * *

Patti was by now similarly tied and gagged at her own chair. Buzz had come and gone, and, at one point, fixed a plate of food, set it on a tray and disappeared. Her bladder screamed to relieve itself, but here she was, tied to a chair in an old cabin with a stranger beside her.

Mental telepathy would come in handy at a time like this, she thought, turning to the man beside her. The fear in his eyes expressed her exact emotion.

What will happen to us? He seemed to ask.

I don't know, she wanted to say, but couldn't. At this point she was simply trying to control her tremors. She wondered how Kim was faring.

Later, Buzz entered the kitchen, soaking wet. He walked directly to her chair and leaned into her face, water dripping onto her lap. "I can't find your damn phone, bitch. You'll pay for this."

CHAPTER EIGHTEEN

The sirens screamed to a halt outside the cabin. Buzz peeked through the dirty kitchen window curtains. Twilight had fallen, but there was just enough light to make out the two patrol cars. "Damn!" he said, and rushed to the kitchen table and pushed it aside exposing the trap door. "You're going down," he said to the two hostages.

He flung the door open, only to hear Kim call out.

"Patti! Is that you?"

"Shut up, chink. Your friends are coming down."

Patti and the stranger glanced at each other. Her flesh prickled. She assumed it was the basement, and just when help was so near! She tried to call out, but the gag was tight and just the attempt to make sound sent her into a round of coughing that she thought would be her end. She was desperate for a deep breath. Her eyes watered, tears of strain ran down her cheeks, and she fought the urge to vomit, terrified she would choke.

Buzz untied the ropes around their legs and torsos one by one, tying their hands behind their backs. "Get on down there," he said, "and don't make a sound. One peep out of you, and I'll blast those cops away."

Idiot. Fat chance of calling for help with this gag on. Patti was the first on the stairway, and terrified of falling. She took the steps sideways one at a time, her only guide the dim light from the kitchen. Next came the stranger, even more slowly judging by the sound of his footsteps on the stairs. The cellar was dark—very dark. The basement was oddly humid and cool, with a constant drip, drip, drip echoing about. She thought she heard running water.

Bam! The trap door slammed shut above them. Now it was truly pitch black.

"Patti...Patti, where are you?" A light flashed into her eyes. "Thank God you're here!" Kim said, then scoped the area quickly with the light until it fell upon the stranger, who stood looking just as terrified as he had when they first saw him.

"Umph! Umph!" the only sounds that Patti could emit.

"My phone, I forgot I had it. Gotta be careful. The battery is half gone. I tried calling out, but no service down here." He turned off the light. "My arm is awful, Patti. Hurts like the devil. I've lost a lot of blood...stay in one place, because I'm coming to you, so don't move." Once he felt the soft flesh of her arm, he used his good hand to pick at the gag's knot at the back of her head. It was knotted tightly, but soon, it loosened, and he pushed it down around her neck.

"Thank God you have a light and a good arm, Kim. See if you can free my hands."

Mission accomplished, though with many attempts. Kim flashed the light once more to the stranger, whose eyes changed from terrified to relief as they approached. Once free to speak, he did.

"That son-of-bitch is a lunatic!" he said.

"No arguing that, mister," Patti said, untying his hands,

"Can't you leave that light on, buddy?" the stranger asked.

"Gotta preserve the battery. Sorry."

"What's your name?" Patti asked. "How'd you get in Buzz's house."

"I'm Richard Bandoff."

"The construction guy?" Kim asked.

"Yes."

"Then that's your Cadillac at the construction site, right?" Patti asked.

"Yes, it is. I wanted to visit Mr. Abbot—not knowing he was off his rocker—to see if he was interested in selling some of his land. He literally flipped out, and slugged me in the eye. I fell, and next thing I know I have a rifle pointed at me. You know the rest. How're we gonna get out of here? That's what I want to know."

"I think I know where we are. Take a look, Patti." Kim flashed the light again. "Look at the pipes," he said, referring to the semicircular row of pipes that Buzz and his father had placed for protection from Snapper so many years ago.

"What in the world...?" Bandoff said. "Is this a cave?"

"Oh, my God, Kim. This is where the tunnel ends!"

"You know what that means."

"I do. It's either in here with us, or out in the river. Those bars are to keep it at bay. I wonder when this was built?"

"What the hell are you two talking about?" Bandoff asked. "What's in here—or not?"

Kim flipped off the light. "You may not want to know, sir."

* * *

Matt sat in the patrol car, Patti's phone in hand. "I can't stop thinking how lucky we were to find this." He spoke to fellow diver, Don Brody, who sat beside him in the back seat. "I'm glad you're here," he added. "Two divers missing, and now Patti and Kim."

"I'm as anxious as you are to find out what's going on. I know that phone wasn't there before, unless it was covered in muck and we just missed it."

"No chance, not with the photos dated today. I can't reach Patti or Kim. For some reason she photo'd the insertion holes for the pipes. I don't know who the Cadillac belongs to, but it's odd how that photo was taken not long before the pipe hole photos."

The two officers who had driven them to Buzz's cabin were standing at the kitchen door under the yellow glow of a porch light waiting for a reply. The door opened, and Buzz stood in the doorway. Matt watched as the officers entered his house.

"They've gone in," Matt said. "Maybe we should at least get out of the car in case they need us."

"They told us to stay here."

"I know, but I don't trust this guy. I'm getting out. Come on. We'll stay by the car."

Matt checked his watch every few minutes. Ten minutes...twelve...fifteen, then twenty. "I hope nothing is wrong." Just as he was about to approach the cabin in search of the officers, the screen door opened and one officer returned. "We've checked the house and it's clear."

"Aren't you going to arrest him?"

"We have nothing on him."

"How about a crazy cave cage to keep a plug-ugly giant freak of a monster in or out of the river?"

"It's his land, sir. We need a crime, or we can't hold him. We have no proof of this…uh…monster yet."

At that moment, the screen door squeaked open again and the other officer returned. "Nothing there," he said. "The man let us search without a warrant."

"What about the missing people? Two scientists and two divers?" Don asked.

"Right," Matt said. "Four people missing and you're doing nothing?"

"Sir, the missing divers will be investigated, but as for the couple, it hasn't even been 24 hours. You're talking about two adults. They could have run off to Vegas together, for all we know. Is this woman your wife?"

"Don't be a smart-ass, and no, no she's not my wife. She's a colleague, and I know damn well she and her partner are in serious trouble."

"I'm sorry, but until we have some evidence, our hands are tied. We can't do a thing. The man's house was clean, and he gave us permission to look around."

"What about the cave trap? The mysterious bars? It's suspicious, isn't it? Is it legal to block off caves in a river?"

"Sir, I wish we could satisfy all your questions, but that is not our department. You will need to direct your questions to the appropriate agency. With that, both officers entered the car and waited for Matt and Don to do the same.

"We may have to take this into our own hands, for speed's sake, Don."

"Agreed, buddy. I'm ready when you are."

CHAPTER NINETEEN

"Hold this, right here." Patti said to Bandoff, handing him Kim's phone, the flashlight aimed at Kim's bare arm. "Let's check out the wound."

"Careful!" Kim warned, grimacing as Patti removed the ragged piece of tee shirt Kim was able to tear off earlier in an attempt to stop the bleeding. "You can't imagine what I went through to get that crappy piece of cloth, what with one good arm. I'm surprised I have any teeth left."

Pattie checked front and back of his upper arm. "Lucky you," she said. "It appears the bullet went straight through. Good news. I hope it missed the bone."

"All I know is that it hurts like hell. It hurts, and it's numb at the same time, if that makes any sense."

"What are we going to do now?" Bandoff asked. "He must need some antiseptic or antibiotics, and we need to get the hell out of this place, whatever it is." He moved the light away from Patti and Kim to aim at the tunnel that curved and disappeared around a bend. "Look, why can't we take that tunnel there?"

"I guess you haven't heard, huh?" Kim asked.

"Heard what?"

"Shine the damn light over here, would you?" Patti asked.

The light returned to Kim's wound, and she retied the shabby bandage.

"What is it I haven't heard about?"

"The monster." Kim said.

"What monster?"

Patti took the phone from Bandoff and shut off the light. "I hate to tell you this, but there is a very large and dangerous creature on the loose."

"What'd'ya mean, a 'creature'?"

"You have to see it to beli...." Kim started, but Patti shut him up and took a deep breath.

"Somehow, an alligator snapper has grown to unbelievable size and, it's killing people. We believe that Buzz, the man upstairs, is involved in this somehow. Also, we think that the tunnel over there leads to the river; and Buzz, believe it or not, has barred off the tunnel entrance. We don't know if the creature is in here with us, or out in the river." There, she said it.

Bandoff was quiet a moment before speaking. "You people are as crazy as the guy upstairs. I've had my crew here for weeks and we haven't seen any giant turtle, for Christ's sake."

"It's true," Kim said. "It's true, and it's a horror to see in person. Three of us have seen it and lived to tell the tale. Others have died, disappeared."

Bandoff grunted. "Bunch of loonies," he said.

It was impossible to see his expression, or look each other in the eye as there was no adjusting to the darkness; it was black as pitch in all directions.

"We need to get control of this situation," Patti said. Why don't we find a place to sit and talk it out? We need to overpower Buzz the next time we see him."

"*If* we see him," Bandoff added.

"Let's think positive!" Pattie said. "We're not giving up. The police were here and maybe they noticed something. Maybe they're still up there. How could they miss the trap door when it's as plain as day if you happen to be looking around?"

"*If* they happen to be looking around."

"Cool it, Mr. Bandoff," Kim said. "Why don't you join our team so we can get out of here?"

"Shine your light a moment," Patti said. "Let's find a place to sit. First, though, I need to hide behind something for, uh, personal reasons." Patti was desperate by this time, and having finally having the chance to relieve her bursting bladder, she felt her way back to the designated pow-wow spot and sat. "Any ideas yet?" she asked. The ground was hard and damp, even slimy. They'd have to be careful not to slip and fall. Kim's injury was enough to deal with.

"How about this," Kim said. When he opens that door, we don't say a word. We make him come down here looking for us, and then we jump him. We can hide on either side of the stairs."

"He'll have a flashlight and see us," Bandoff said.

"We'll hide *under* the stairwell, then."

"We can try," Patti said.

But Buzz didn't return, and the plan was untried. Hours passed. The hostages attempted sleep, but the ground was beyond uncomfortable. The damp and coolness of the cavern air seeped into their bones after such an extended time, leaving them chilled.

Pattie woke from a fitful few minutes of shut-eye, sat up and pushed a button on her wristwatch. The battery had been depleting for a while, and with the tragedy of losing Ted, and the chaos of the discovery of the creature, she had not replaced it. But, in the pitch black, the dimming light of the watch glowed momentarily. It seemed a blessing. "3:20," she said.

"A.M. or P.M.?" Kim asked.

"You're awake."

"Are you kidding? What else would I be doing in this Godforsaken hole?"

"I assume it's a.m. since it was late afternoon when we arrived."

"I can't wait to get my hands on that guy," Bandoff said. "He's probably up there having sweet dreams while we're freezing to death in a cavern with no food or water. I'm thirsty."

"Me too," Kim said. "I heard running water."

"I heard it too, but I don't know if we should follow the sound," Patti said.

"Well, I don't care what you think. I'm not planning on dying of thirst in this hellhole." Bandoff stood, with difficulty, judging from the grunts it took to get his stocky body off the cavern floor. "Gimme that light. I'll check it out,"

"No way," Kim said. "This is all we've got aside from Patti's puny wrist watch light."

"Then get off your ass and come with me."

"How about you, Patti?" Kim asked.

"I don't know…we're pretty easy targets if we leave the barrier."

"Stay here if you want. I'm going, light or no light." Bandoff said.

"We haven't seen *it* yet," Kim said. "Maybe it's locked out, and not trapped in here?"

"Oh, jeez. I don't know. Buzz is probably sleeping and won't be down here till morning. Okay," she said after a moment's silence. "I'll come." She rose off the floor and automatically reached out in the darkness to feel for Kim. "Let's hold onto each other."

Single file, Kim in front, Patti in the middle and Bandoff in the rear, they followed the brief flashes of Kim's light to guide them out of the safety zone, weaving around the stalactites and stalagmites.

"Now shush! Listen!" Patti ordered, once beyond the vertical bars.

With all silent, in the dark distance they heard the water running. "The tunnel," she said. "Flash your light a moment."

With the tunnel viewed ahead, Kim put the flashlight to rest and they proceeded, running their hands along the damp wall for guidance.

"It feels different here," Patti said after a while. "More open. The light, Kim."

They gasped—the three of them— as the light fell upon the grand chamber of the cavern, its stalactites and stalagmites rising and hanging in magnificent jaw-dropping splendor.

Kim quickly did a once around with the light. "The creature's not here, Patti, but look! There's the river!"

With water in sight, their thirst overcame the fear of the beast. They ran to the cavern's river, and once there, Kim turned off the light, satisfied they had nothing to worry about at the moment.

They knelt, bringing handfuls of cool water to their lips.

"Water never tasted so good!" Patti said, having quenched her thirst. "At least we have this."

Kim turned the light on again to see where the river led. "Should we go on a ways?"

"Yes!" Bandoff piped in. Maybe we can get out of here."

"No chance unless you can hold your breath a while."

"Why?"

"Eventually this air pocket ends into a full blown river, water top to bottom at its entrance, and we have no idea how long it runs. We didn't have a chance to investigate."

"We could walk a ways. How's your flashlight battery?"

"Less than half."

The trio moved along the narrow riverside walkway guided by feeling their way along the damp wall. Kim's light exposed the expanse of the tunnel, and he and Patti agreed that it was certainly wide enough for the beast to move through. Kim used the light frugally, turning it off a few minutes, and then turning it on again briefly. The view did not change, aside from the occasional bend in the river.

"How far do you think we've gone?" Bandoff asked.

"Far enough, I'd sa...." A "clunk" and rolling sound stopped the trio in their tracks. "Wait. I hit something. What is it?" Kim said. He shined the light to his feet.

"A flashlight!" Patti said excitedly, reaching to grasp the object that was a hair's breadth from falling into the river. She flicked it on. "It works! Alleluia! But, you know what? I wonder if this light belonged to one of the cave divers that went missing."

"A mixed blessing," Kim said, flicking off his light. "I'm turning the phone off now. We'll save it for a phone call if we can ever get a signal down here."

Patti pointed the flashlight ahead toward the flow of the river. "It's getting wider and deeper. Look, we'll run out of foot room soon. A few more steps and our shoes would have been wet," Patti added. "Let's turn back." She gave the flashlight to Kim.

They were almost to the Great Way, still excited about the flashlight discovery, when Kim, still in the lead, stopped. "Smell that?" he asked.

Patti sniffed. "Oh, no," she said faintly. Her neck hairs stood on end. "Quick!" she whispered.

"What is it?" Bandoff asked, much too loudly.

"Shut-up, it'll hear you," Kim said.

"What? The giant turtle?" he replied mockingly.

"Yes, the giant turtle, you idiot," Kim said.

"No time for this, get moving!" Patti gave Kim a shove, and they were off in a mad dash for safety.

"Oh, my God, Kim. I can hear it! Hurry!"

Bandoff grabbed ahold of the back of Patti's shirt, as Kim had taken off at a rapid pace. Kim held the light steady ahead, and soon they reached the immense cavern. "Hurry!" he said, and flashed the light toward the tunnel that led to the safety zone.

An explosive hiss and burst of foul air nearly knocked them over as they entered the tunnel. With the light guiding them, they were able to maneuver their way through its curves, to weave in and out of the stalagmites and duck the stalactites until they were able to reach the safety zone. Once there, out of breath and gasping for air, Kim turned the light to the passageway from which they had just come.

"My God!" Bandoff exclaimed. "What is that?"

Snapper's mighty beak chomped at air. He hissed, swung his ugly head, and butt the bars of the safety zone, which, thankfully, only bent a fraction. The odor of river life and low tide permeated the cavern atmosphere as he hissed and moved back and forth along the outside of the bars. His daggered claws scrapped menacingly at the cavern floor as he passed. He was a horrid sight and even more so in the spot of the flashlight. But then, the flashlight flickered.

"Turn it off!" Patti yelled.

Kim obeyed, and at that moment a dim light penetrated the cavern. Eyes turned to the single lightbulb that hung from a string of lights that stretched from the trap door to the passageway that curved out of sight.

Snapper now stood front and center behind the protective bars, regaining their full attention. There was no missing him under the dim light as it made him appear all the more terrifying. Shadows outlined the pits and valleys of his grotesque form as he stood staring at the intruders, exhaling putrid air with such force that it ruffled the hair on their heads as if they were caught in a sudden summer storm. Bandoff stepped backward until he tripped against the bottom of the stairway falling onto the third step. His jaw hung open. "What the hell?"

"Meet Snapper."

All heads turned to see Buzz halfway down the stairway, rifle in hand and pointed straight at Bandoff.

"He's hungry and wants one of you."

"You're crazy, mister," Bandoff said.

"And you're first," Buzz replied.

The color drained from Bandoff's face.

"He was my daddy's pet, way back since the 30's," Buzz said, as if involved in a pleasant conversation. "He grew."

"Let us out of here, Buzz." Patti tried to keep her voice calm. "You can't hide this thing any longer."

"Too late. I can't let you go. Cops didn't find a thing here, and they won't find you."

"You son of a bitch!" Bandoff yelled, crawling the stairs like a spider. Before Buzz realized what was happening, Bandoff had grabbed his foot and yanked, pulling him off balance. Buzz flew off the stairs landing on the cavern floor with a "thump" and a loud exhale of air. The rifle bounced a few feet beyond his reach, but just as Patti ran to grab it, Buzz was quicker. He tripped her, and she flew to the floor on hands and knees. Foiled, she wanted to scream; she wanted to kill the man. In a flash Buzz was on his feet again, rifle in hand.

Patti caught a glimpse of Bandoff as he continued his spider crawl up the stairs. She was alarmed to see Kim, struggling with only one useful arm, trying to follow him. "Hurry!" she screamed; but Buzz knocked Kim off the lower stairs, and he now lay in pain at his feet. Buzz jammed a heavy foot on his belly to hold him, and then aimed at Bandoff, firing the rifle.

Patti and Kim watched as Bandoff's limp body slid down three or four stairs before tumbling the rest of the way. He landed in a heap, dead, shot clean through the head, then came to rest partially on Kim, who still lay imprisoned by Buzz's foot.

"Push him through the bars," Buzz ordered, stepping off of Kim.

Silence.

Buzzed pointed the rifle at Kim's head. "Get up and give him to Snapper. Now!" he yelled.

Patti stood and rushed to Kim's aid. "This is inhumane. The man deserves to be buried, not eaten." They had temporarily forgotten about Snapper in all the commotion, so turned to witness him hiss and blast them again with his putrid breath.

Kim coughed, and Patti winced at the foul air. Buzz stood fast, the rifle aimed at her midriff. "Push him through the bars. Do it!"

"Jesus," Patti mumbled. "Poor guy."

Each took an arm and dragged him timidly toward the barrier. Once there, they knelt; and Kim, with one hand, tried to help Patti push Bandoff's corpse through the bars, but it proved too difficult a task considering the injury to his arm.

"I'll do it," Patti said, wiping a tear from her eye. "What a monster that man is." she whispered. "Just sit back. It's okay." All the while, Snapper stared, his beady black eyes lowered to better watch their actions, his exhalations turning their stomachs sour with the stench.

"I'm scared," Patti whispered, as she attempted to push Bandoff further into Snapper's zone. She was afraid of getting her arms too far past the barrier, and her fears rang true when Snapper clamped his jaws shut just inches from her arm.

"Oh my God!" she yelled, jerking back.

Lucky for her, the job was finished when Snapper pierced Bandoff's midsection with his sharp beak and lifted him high above their heads, dangling like a rag doll.

"I can't stand to look at that thing, much less think what a horror it would be to…."

"Enough!" Patti said, cutting Kim off before he could verbalize his thought. She couldn't bear to think of what poor Ted must have endured.

"I'm sorry." Kim said. "I didn't mean to…."

"It's okay."

As quickly as the light had brightened their dungeon, it darkened it again. They heard the trap door slam shut, and sat in complete darkness listening to Snapper eat his meal.

CHAPTER TWENTY

Matt and Don tread water at the barred entrance to the cavern, along with four other members of the recovery division. To their gear they had added video cameras to their face masks, and power heads for the spear guns.

"We need photos or videos of this thing," Matt had said earlier as he attached his camera. "I'm sure seeing the beast will convert any nay-sayers— if there are any left out there."

"No joke," Don replied.

Now at the precipice of the unknown, they submerged, propelling themselves through the bars of the barricade to enter the unknown territory of the cave.

"We'll find out once and for all where this ends." Matt took the lead, his dive light on, his spear gun loaded.

"Is your camera running?" Don asked.

"You bet," Matt replied.

The dive lights shone eerily ahead, beaming off rough limestone walls that at times expanded into greater spans and then narrowed again, but always wide enough for the beast to pass. Matt pointed to a smaller tunnel. "We'll check that out later."

"No way could the creature fit in that hole," Don replied.

Silence followed as the six divers continued through the underground cavern.

"I hate to admit it, but this is creepy—and amazing," Don said.

Matt replied by raising his free hand in acknowledgement. He slowed after several minutes of leading the team, when ahead loomed a dark curvature of the tunnel. He stopped and signaled the others to do the same.

"What is it? Is it coming?" There was no mistaking the alarm in Don's voice. "Should we go?"

"Just wait," Matt ordered. "The current has changed. Can you feel it?"

All divers had stopped, eyes glued to the curve ahead.

"Let's keep going," Matt said after a brief respite in which the beast did not appear. But just as they reached the darkened curve, Matt's headlamp caught sight of one giant dagger embellished forefoot... then another. As the horrid creature turned the corner, his beady eyes briefly reflected in the dive lights. "Get out of here!" Matt yelled. The sudden light blinded the creature just long enough to give the men a head start back to the cavern entrance.

There was virtually nowhere to hide; no crevices deep enough to protect them from the razor beak and claws of the monster, and no time to aim and shoot. Matt was now at the tail end of the dive team—or so he thought—and his heart pounded heavily as he pumped his finned feet. *"Faster, faster!"* his head screamed. The other divers, except for Don, seemed far ahead, and he wondered if Don was behind him. He didn't dare stop for even a fraction of a second. On and on he went, not remembering having come so far into the tunnel. He knew the beast was close behind. At one point he thought he felt the monster upon him, and was relieved to discover that it was Don, frantically pumping his own legs and, at one time in his panicked state, reaching out to Matt.

"Keep... going..." Matt said, gasping for breath that surely was vanishing quickly from the tanks with the stress and exertion of escaping a sure death. There was no choice to but to keep swimming; that, or be killed in a gruesome fashion.

At last, the steel bars of the opening were in view. Ahead, the other divers swam through like a school of fish. Matt slithered through quickly, and Don was nearly through when the beast clamped down on his finned foot.

"No!" he yelled, as it tried to pull himself through the bars.

Matt quickly grabbed ahold of Don's hands, which were white-knuckling a steel bar. "Don't let him get me!" Don yelled, his eyes large in terror.

"Don't let go! I'm going to spear him!" Matt finned himself backward a few feet and aimed the spear gun, praying it wouldn't stray and hit Don. It didn't. Instead it sank into an algae covered osteoderm on the creature's back. The beast released Don's foot, extended his snake-like neck, and removed the spear with his beak. He then lunged his head through the bars trying to recapture his prey, but it was too late. Don was safely through.

A trail of blood from Don's injured foot followed the divers as they quickly swam downriver and out of the beast's vision. Matt pulled Don along with one hand, as he seemed incapable of keeping with the group. The "thuds" of the creature banging against the iron bars of his prison resonated throughout the depths of the river, riding the current and causing the minnow schools to dart and dash to the thumps of his dilemma. Matt wondered how long it would take for it to break through the gate.

By the time the team reached home base, oxygen levels were nearing depletion. Don was weak, as he had lost a lot of blood on the return swim. Matt quickly removed his equipment, along with Don's. When he attempted to remove the damaged fin, Don howled in pain, and Matt could see why. Don's foot was nearly severed at the ankle! On the inside of the ankle, bone protruded through ragged, raw flesh.

"Don't look, buddy. Ambulance is on the way."

* * *

"That didn't go so well, did it." Don mumbled later, laying prone on the ambulance stretcher.

"Guess I'm a lousy shot," Matt replied.

"Why? Were you aiming for his head?"

"Hell, no, I was aiming for you—put you out of your misery."

Don managed a weak grin. "I figured. Seriously, though, your hit saved my life. Thanks, pal. We didn't get very far though, did we?"

"Don't you worry about it; your job is to get your foot taken care of."

"I wanted to help...you...." Don's eyes closed as the administered pain drugs took effect.

With Don stabilized, the ambulance crew prepared to leave for the hospital. Matt watched until the flashing red lights were no longer visible through the dense forest. The small, muddy ramp was crowded now with the four other divers, the state police, and local authority, including George March, the mayor of Riverside.

The recovery divers were very animated in their description of the massive creature, or, of what they witnessed in the short glimpse before terror took hold. The old expression rang true: "four people saw an elephant—or in this case, monster—four different ways", as each diver interpreted his glimpse of the creature differently.

Matt overheard one diver speaking with another. "I never had to dive for something like this, and I don't know if I want to get anywhere near it again." He could relate to that comment. Neither did he, but it was his job.

The sun now headed down beyond the trees with twilight soon to follow. The beast was trapped—hopefully—but still, there were the two missing divers along with Patti and Kim. Matt rummaged through his equipment for the video camera. He was sure he caught at least the forefeet and the head of the beast before hightailing it in the escape.

"I can clarify this," Matt said, retrieving the full face communication mask. If he captured the beast in a photo, then the authorities would have an idea of what they were up against. He froze; the camera that had been attached to the headgear was missing

A rustle in the bushes nearby caused everyone on the dirt ramp to jump in alarm. A light flashed, momentarily blinding the group, and then the slight figure of a man approached.

"Riverside Times, folks. Maybe you can enlighten the fine people of this state as to what's going on around here?"

"Get out of here, Chet," the mayor said.

"No way. Sheriff Monroe vanishes, "no swimming, fishing, or boating signs" are posted up and down the river, not to mention state troopers and scuba divers swarming the place. I think the good citizens deserve to know what the big hubbub is about."

Deputy Dave, temporarily sworn in as sheriff, stepped forward. "Listen, Chet. We have a serious situation going on here. There's no need to spread panic at the moment."

"Sorry Dave, but I'm a newsman and this smells like an important story."

"Can't you arrest him for...for something?" Mayor March asked.

Dave shrugged.

"For Christ's sake, Dave, use your authority!" The mayor ordered.

"I...I...."

"Who the hell elected you as useless sheriff?" Mayor March blasted.

Witnessing Dave's embarrassment and the stagnant standoff, Matt stepped forward. "Let me help here," Matt said, turning to Chet. "We can promise you this: you will get an exclusive on the story, in full, and photos, if you keep quiet for now. Not a word in the papers. Not a word whispered or leaked. Deal?"

Perhaps it was the tall, muscular figure of a man, still dressed in the black scuba suit overshadowing the much slighter newsman, which brought about the agreement between the men on the shore and the man with the camera, but an agreement was made; Chet would remain silent as long as he was promised the entire story.

CHAPTER TWENTY-ONE

"Kim," Patti whispered. "Are you awake?"

After Snapper had finished his meal of Mr. Bandoff, the sound of his departure was of great relief compared to the grisly sound of him chomping through bone and flesh. Perhaps from shock— or exhaustion— the pair remained silent after crawling as far away from the iron bars, and Snapper's deadly beak, as possible. Words were not spoken until this moment.

Kim groaned. "Yeah, I'm awake now. Guess I fell asleep. I was hoping this was just a nightmare."

"We both slept. My watch has stopped working, so I have no idea how much time as elapsed since...since...."

"I know. Don't say it! I'm trying to forget."

"We have to get out of here, Kim. Either we ambush Buzz successfully the next time we see him, or we follow the river. One way or another, we have to make an attempt."

"I agree. Just wish my arm would stop pounding so I could be more helpful. It really hurts, Patti. It hurts *bad*."

"I know Kim...I just want to kill that guy." She had never felt as helpless as she was now. Kim needed medical care. The longer they waited, the better the possibility of infection. "Is the flashlight working?" she asked.

A dim and narrow beam of light bounced to the right and left and settled on her face. "You look like hell, Patti."

"Shut up. Turn it off. Save the battery, what's left of it. How about the phone?"

"I think it has a bit of a charge. I don't want to turn it on until we really need it."

"Brainstorm time. Let's get a plan going."

* * *

Matt and a new dive buddy, Steve, geared up in the shallow waters of home base. Dawn was just breaking, giving the divers plenty of daylight time in which to search. With the event of Don's injury the day before, a pow-wow with the mayor and other officials was to be held at 10:00 a.m. at the sheriff's department in town. More divers were expected to aid in the rescue; but first, the red tape must be dealt with.

Matt could not wait for the red tape. He needed to find the camera, and most of all, the two missing divers as well as Patti and Kim. He stuffed two power heads into his vest pocket, gave two to Steve, and both men were supplied with dual steel oxygen tanks. Without knowing where the cavern tunnel ended, and with the beast trapped within, they had to be prepared.

At the gate of the cavern, the men stopped the swim. Matt instructed Steve to search for the camera on the outside, which they did; but with no luck, they swam through the bars searching the muddy bottom within the limestone entryway.

"Further." Matt pointed ahead, and they swam close to the bottom scanning the area for the missing camera. Matt did not hesitate to shine his headlamp ahead every few seconds checking for the beast's return.

They continued through the craggy cave until they reached the point where the beast had turned the corner and their hasty retreat to the entryway had begun. "We haven't been past this point," Matt said. "Let's keep going." He checked his GPS and was amazed at the twists and turns their journey had taken.

"How the heck far does this thing go?" Steve asked.

"Don't know, but we're going to find out, with any luck."

At one point, the cavern deepened into a larger cavern with wider and higher walls, and then inclined to a shallower depth. Soon, their fins touched bottom.

"Will you look at this!" Steve exclaimed as the men peeked above the surface. The river had narrowed considerably at this point, and meandered off to the right, disappearing behind magnificent stalagmites, swirled and marbled in design, rocketing upward from the cavern floor as if reaching to meet the potpourri of incredible and breathtaking stalactites that pitched downward into the abyss.

"Amazing," Matt replied in awe. "So this is where he lives." Matt's headlamp scanned the great cavern, feeling as if they had entered the jaws of a monstrous, but stunning, beast. That thought brought to mind the reality of the situation—*dangerous*—as their only visibility was delivered by the dive lights, and they had entered an unknown world. There was no turning back.

"Let's put the tanks on the edge, there," Matt said, removing his heavy and cumbersome dive gear. His voice seemed strange to himself, hollowed and slightly echoed. It lifted and morphed, blending into the dank and spacious atmosphere of the cavern, traveling the high perimeters until it vanished into some unseen jagged nook.

With their equipment piled on the river's edge, the men removed their headgear as well, and then the dive lights from the helmets, snapping them onto their wrist mounts. They kept the spear guns with them, along with the powerheads for safety measures.

"The beast must be here, somewhere," Matt said, reducing his voice to a whisper. "He could be anywhere." He shone his light full circle and into many dark crevices and passageways. One passage was very wide, disappearing around a craggy bend. "First, let's see where the river goes."

They followed the dive lights along the river, bending and side-stepping to avoid the occasional stalagmites. All was quiet except for the drip, drip, drip of the endless deposit of rain water that filtered from the ground level above, to mix with minerals in the rock and limestone. This perpetual precipitation created the wondrous vision that embraced them in this amazing discovery of an underworld.

"Oh, oh." Matt said, stopping to shine his dive light onto a few scattered objects. "Oh, my God, no." he said beneath his breath.

Steve's dive light met with Matt's on the unfortunate discovery, a bloodied arm, sparsely covered with torn pieces of black Neoprene[ii], the same as the suits they wore at this moment. Next to it, a fin.

Matt turned and scanned their surroundings, feeling jarred by the debris of which he assumed were remnants of a missing diver, and not Patti and Kim.

"Let's get out of here," Steve said.

"Not yet. That beast could be anywhere, but I have a feeling he may be down this direction, near the food source. We can't leave until we look for the others. Let's try that large passageway on the other side, away from this gruesome mess."

"You got it," Steve said and followed Matt across a great expanse to the larger tunnel that turned into the unknown.

With trepidation, they followed their dive lights, mindful always of any signal indicating that the monster may be near.

* * *

"Kim," Patti whispered. "I heard something. I think it's coming!"

They scooched across the floor until they felt the stairway, then scooched beneath the stairwell.

"Don't forget to breathe," Patti said, more of a reminder to herself, as she needed to feel that Kim was with her— that she was not alone in this nightmare— and that they were still amongst the living. Against any control, she began to tremble, wishing she could forget the sound of Mr. Bandoff being eaten, forget that this is most likely what happened to Ted and the other divers, that this could happen to both her and Kim if they couldn't escape.

"Look at the tunnel," Kim whispered, waking her from the morbid thoughts she couldn't shake. "I see a light. How'd Buzz get there?"

"Shhh…," she said, as they both crouched, peeking through the second and third treads of the stairway.

"How'd he get past…."

"Quiet!" she whispered. And then recognition struck as the two men with dive lights entered into view. "Matt! It's Matt, look!" Then, thinking the worst could happen, that Snapper should scoop their rescuers up, she stood, bumping her head on the stairs above. "Get out of there!" she yelled, rubbing her crown. In passing, she thought her bump felt moist, but the fact that her head may be bleeding was only secondary to the relief she felt at seeing the possibility of rescue.

"Hurry up!" Kim yelled. "It's in here—*somewhere*…."

* * *

"Well, our friend Buzz must hold stock in the Steel industry," Matt said as he and Steve perused the semi-circle of steel bars. "He went to great lengths to hide the creature from the world and apparently from himself, too."

"According to Buzz, he and his father built this safety zone decades ago to keep Snapper away," Patti said.

"Snapper? The thing has a name?"

"He started out as a pet turtle, according to Buzz's story." Patti continued.

"But he *grew*," Kim piped in.

"Sure did," Steve said beneath his breath.

Sitting in a circle, the dive lights bouncing off the cavern walls, Patti and Kim relayed their capture by Buzz, Kim's bullet wound, and the horrifying scene when Mr. Bandoff was murdered and fed to Snapper.

"You wouldn't happen to have any pain killers on you, would you?" Kim asked "My arm is killing me."

"Sorry buddy. But we'll get you out of here and to a hospital."

"Before I get gangrene, I hope."

"We think we've found the remains of at least one of the divers." Matt said.

"No doubt. Snapper is a horrid beast. We've been close enough to be his next meal. I don't know how we're going to get out of here. Buzz has the rifle, and we have nothing."

"Hey, you have us," Steve offered.

"I'm sorry," Patti said. "It's been very stressful down here in the dark. We don't know what time it is, or what day, for that matter."

"Near as I can tell, you've been missing for two days," Matt said. "And it's 10:20 a. m. according to my watch."

"Let's try the trap door." Matt stood, with Steve following. "You two stay put. If Buzz is up there, we can handle him."

At the top of the stairs Matt braced his shoulder against the door, but it didn't budge. "Guess we need force," he said, and Steve squeezed next to him on the narrow tread. With shoulders pinned against the door, they pushed, but to no avail.

"Okay, let's give it a whack. Ready?" They both bent their knees, counted to three and heaved upward, their shoulders banging hard against the locked door. It budged, slightly.

"Again," Matt said, and again they banged against the door. It budged again, and more so. "The lock is coming loose. Keep going."

With knees bent and at the count of two, a gunshot blasted a hole through the door, missing Matt's ear by a fraction.

"Jesus!" Steve said, and scrambled down the steps.

"You can't get away with this, Buzz. Open up. Game's over."

"That's what you think, chink."

"He thinks it's me!" Kim whispered.

Matt crept down the stairs. "Chink?"

"That's what he calls me. Nice fellow."

"Let's let him think it's you for the time being."

Another shell blasted through the trap door, and the group scattered to the edge of the bars. "Don't try it again!" Buzz yelled.

"Christ, that guy's serious!" Steve said. "What now? We're between a rock and a hard place."

The group breathed a sigh of relief when it appeared Buzz had stopped firing. The trap door remained shut.

"I have an idea," Matt said. "That is, if the bea...*Snapper*...leaves us alone."

"What is it? We have to try *something* to get out of here." Patti again reached up to feel what was now a large bump on the top of her head. "Ouch! Shine that light over here a moment."

Matt obliged, and when Patti looked at her fingers, they were covered in a sticky red. "It was my excitement of seeing you guys. I bumped it on the stairwell; but make no mistake, it won't keep me from attempting any plan you come up with. Kim is much more seriously injured."

"Think you can make it, buddy?" Matt asked.

"Exactly what is the plan?" Kim replied.

"We make a dash for it, back through that huge cavern. Steve and I don our equipment. We swim until we lose the airspace, then we air-share. I'm sure you've practiced the emergency procedure."

"Yes… but with full face masks? That's going to make it nearly impossible."

"Not impossible, just more difficult."

Kim shuddered. "This goes from worse to worse, if that's possible. And what about Snapper? We've seen him in action, and it isn't pleasant."

"It's a gamble, but the best we can do at this point. We have spear guns and power heads if necessary. And, we each have dual tanks."

"Dual tanks, or no, with a long tunnel, exertion and full-face mask air share, I don't see much hope on survival," Patti said.

"It's either that, or wait for Buzz to let us out of here, and by the looks of it, I don't think he's planning on that."

"Were there any air pockets in the tunnel?" Patti asked.

"There may have been, but we didn't stop to check, or utilize any."

Patti shook her head. It couldn't get worse than this. Either way, danger and death lurked in all directions.

"Okay," she said, after much thought. "I'm game."

"Me too," Kim dittoed reluctantly. "But these may be my last moments on earth, and a sad few, if I may add: a shot-up arm, a monster on the loose, and the possibility of drowning in an underwater cave, or being eaten alive. This is not the way I planned to go."

"Nobody asked me if I was game," Steve said.

"Three to one, pal."

"Just joking. Let's go blast our way to turtle glory."

CHAPTER TWENTY-TWO

With Matt in the lead and Steve taking up the rear, Patti and Kim were nestled in between the men as they made their way single file through the passageway to the Great Way. Matt shined his light around the perimeter in search of Snapper. "Where the heck can he be?" he whispered.

"All I know is that I'm dying of thirst."

"Kim's right. We desperately need water," Patti said. "Take us to the river, first."

Once there, Patti and Kim fell to their knees and scooped water into their hands repeatedly until their thirst was satisfied. All the while, Matt and Steve scanned their surroundings for any sign of Snapper.

"Alligator snappers like to stay wet," she said, wiping the water from her chin. Now that he's trapped, he may know another way out. After all, this river has to come from somewhere."

"Let's hope that's the case," Matt replied. "Let's see if we can get out of here before he shows up."

Patti slipped out of her jeans. "Can't swim in denim so I'm in my undies now. Hey, get that light off of me!"

"Oops—sorry. " At the first sound of her voice, Matt had aimed his headlight on her, but quickly removed it at her barking order.

"Consider it a bikini bottom. I can't have a wet pair of jeans dragging me down. You'd better do the same, Kim."

"This isn't easy with one arm, you know," Kim said, apparently struggling to disrobe.

"Need help?" Matt asked.

"No…I'll get it. There. Done."

Patti's legs, feeling the cool air of the cave, grew goosebumps. She shivered, and then, with growing horror, sniffed the dank air. "Oh, no."

"What?" Kim asked, and then, "Oh, my God. He's here!"

"Get out of there, and hurry!" Patti said, to the two men who stood waist high in water ready to don their equipment.

They shined their lights in every direction looking for the beast. "We've got to hide somewhere." Matt said.

Patti grabbed his wrist. "Point the light over that way. I think I saw something."

Sure enough, the light rested on a narrow crevice. "I hope it's deep enough," Matt said.

The group moved as one, stepping backward, all eyes following the lights that repeatedly scanned the perimeter of the Great Way.

"I can smell it now," Steve said.

"He's closer," Patti said. "He knows we're here. They have a remarkable sense of smell."

"And sight," Kim added.

Twenty feet from the crevice, Snapper barreled into view. He hissed, his foul breath and body reeking of death. He lumbered toward the group, who stood highlighted by their own dive lights. His claws scraping against the limestone and rock floor as he gained speed.

"Run for it!" Matt yelled, and the group dove into the crevice, clawing their way into the narrow space.

Snapper's breath permeated the crevice which, though narrow, was blessedly deep and wide enough for the group to turn and face their enemy.

"Jesus," Steve said, gagging. "Damn thing stinks!"

Matt shined his light toward Snapper, only to scooch backward as one powerful claw reached in nearly far enough to pierce his wrist. Snapper hissed and withdrew, and then lowered his head to peer into the crevice.

"Damn thing," Matt whispered.

"Jeez," Patti said, lowering her head to rest on her arms. She suppressed a sob that threatened to explode. She was tired and scared to death. Kim was seriously hurt, and it appeared there was no way out. "What the hell do we do now?"

* * *

They waited…and waited…and waited, while Snapper paced and hissed, disturbed over his inability to catch the trespassers. Just the sound of his claws scrapping across the cavern floor sent shivers up Patti's spine. After what seemed like hours, during which Matt and Steve had turned off the dive lights leaving them in total darkness, the sounds of Snapper departing reached their ears. As sounds and smell of the beast faded away, and all that was heard was the drip, drip, drip of the stalactites, Matt turned on his dive light and scanned the Great Way. "I think he's gone. But where?" he whispered.

"We didn't hear any splashing, so perhaps he didn't go into the river," Patti said.

"Let's make a swim for it. What do you say, Matt?" Steve asked.

"Let's make sure first," Matt replied.

The two divers crawled from the crevice, scanning the area with the dive lights. "All clear," Matt informed Patti and Kim quietly. They, too, emerged from the crevice, and when all four stood together, they made their way to the section of the river where Matt and Steve had first arrived.

"Hurry, get your gear," Matt whispered.

They entered the river as quietly as humanly possible. Pattie and Kim stood guard as the men donned their equipment. "Still clear," Patti said intermittently, while praying the men would hurry. She was certain—or was she?—that there had been no sounds of splashing when Snapper left the crevice. She *hoped* this was so and that their swim to safety would be uneventful. But he was a crafty beast. She had no idea how far they would swim before the emergency procedure of air sharing would begin, and how long it would be required. "How long is the tunnel?" she asked.

"Maybe a mile," Matt whispered. "Not sure, but a lot of it is under water."

"Great," Kim said. I don't see how I can make it with this arm."

"I know it's not easy to swallow, Kim, but we have to try. The main thing is, *don't panic*. If you panic, we're dead. You'll have to trust me, buddy. That's the deal. You don't need to do anything except use your good arm. I'm going to hold the mask to your face when the time comes for your two breaths."

"Okay then, we're ready, Matt said.

"First, we're going piggy back, so climb on," Steve submerged and Kim gripped—with his good hand— Steve's shoulder and they took off, gliding to the power of Steve's fins.

Patti took ahold of Matt's shoulders, as well, and they too glided the river, Matt below, and she above, her head above water. Being in the rear with the thought that they would be the first victims of attack should Snapper discover them, bristled her neck hairs. She struggled to concentrate instead on what lie ahead when emergency procedures became necessary. Either choice of thought was enough to bring on a panic attack.

It seemed too short a distance before air sharing was required. Patti fought the panic that overtook her when Steve stopped ahead, treading water, with Kim resting his one good arm on his shoulder. "This is it," Steve said.

"If this tunnel is a mile, then we have a long way to go yet," Patti replied, looking ahead to where the water's surface met the cave ceiling.

"Don't panic. Don't think about it. Our goal is to get out alive. It will be alright if you *don't panic*. Remember, two breaths, and share the air. " Matt was doing his best to console her, but she knew the odds; air sharing was difficult and awkward at best, and with a full face mask for such a long distance, it seemed nearly impossible. She could only hope that there were pockets of air ahead. This would be the test of a lifetime—literally.

"Keep your nerves in check and we'll be fine." Steve's voice sounded hollow as it bounced off the jagged cavern walls. Though well intended, it was, instead, an ominous prelude to an ominous journey of which the outcome was left totally to luck and the ability to suppress panic.

Matt undid the straps that held the mask to his face. "Okay, listen up." His words were choppy as he continued to tread water. "Side by side, okay? Two breaths, and switch. Two breaths and switch. Remain calm and we'll make it. Whatever you do, don't struggle. You *will* have air."

"I hate that beast…" were Patti's last words before Matt submerged, pulling her down with him. He immediately put the mask to her face as she held onto his waist with both hands. *Two breaths, two breaths,* she reminded herself. *Don't panic!* When Matt retrieved the mask, putting it to his own face, she felt the beginning of full blown panic. It bloomed inside her stomach and crept in sinister fashion up her throat. *Don't panic! Two breaths, two breaths!* Matt's fins beat slowly at the water as they covered the distance…three feet…five feet… ten feet and on. Slowly she recovered her fear as they glided like jellyfish through the tunnel; two breaths for him, two for her. She wondered how Kim was faring but didn't dare take her eyes from Matt. It was what kept her calm, his being so near and in such remarkable control of whatever he was experiencing, even though she was sure this was a struggle for him as well. She felt silly. She was a trained scuba diver. She swam with whales, sharks, sting rays, barracuda; but never had she been in a situation where she had to air share with a full face mask while being hunted by a monstrous freak of nature!

Concentrating so intently on her breathing, she did not notice that they had entered a much larger area than the tunnel. In her mesmerized state of mind, thinking only of the two allotted breaths and drifting forward like plankton in a vast sea, the sudden and swift current below did not register alarm. It was when Matt's body jerked suddenly that her eyes grew big. Matt thrust the mask to her face and pulled her upward until her head bumped against the cavern ceiling. Crooking her neck until her head lay sideways on her shoulder, she discovered a few precious inches of air. This way, she and Matt faced one another, as absurd creatures whose only view of life was at this angle.

"The beast is here." he whispered. "Cling to the wall." His voice was distorted, and out of sheer stress and terror she wanted to laugh. She wanted to laugh at their comical positions, the sound of his voice struggling up a severely crooked windpipe at this life-death situation. Instead, her body erupted in trembles so severe she thought for sure they would close her throat, as it was difficult enough to keep still clinging to what little she could of the sharp and jagged wall of the cavern without moving her legs for buoyancy, fighting the river current, and with her head in such an unnatural angle.

"The others?" she managed to spit out.

"Don't know," he answered. "Be still."

When the all too familiar, rough carapace brushed by her vertical figure and pushed her hips against the wall, she wanted to scream. "He hit me!" she whispered, choking on the words.

Certain that Snapper would return and grab her with his sharp beak, she closed her eyes tight and waited for death. Surely Snapper knew she was there; surely he sensed their presence. Then, in the distance, she heard a splash, a grunt.

"What was that? Was that them?"

"I don't know," Matt whispered. "Be still."

"Oh, my God," she said, the panic rising again in her chest. She fought against it, inch by inch as it crept upward. She thought of diving under, getting it over with. It was the waiting that was killing her.

Several minutes passed before Matt said "Let's try it again." He pulled her under and they set off, side by side, *two breaths, two breaths....*

* * *

Recalling the brief sounds they had heard earlier while clinging to the cavern wall, Patti glanced quickly ahead while Matt took in his two breaths. *Where are Steve and Kim?* Visibility was fair, but made poorer by the fact that she had no mask to protect her eyes. The brief glance was totally unproductive, and the exertion of that one small move only stole the oxygen she needed to hold in her lungs while waiting for her turn of the mask. Still, she could not help but wonder how they fared; did the strange sound they heard have something to do with Steve and Kim and their wellbeing? Did Snapper...*stop!* Allowing her mind to wander from the one goal of air share could be deadly! Every inch of distance covered required total concentration; *two breaths. Two breaths...two breaths.*

Regardless of the air share, she began to feel lightheaded. *When does this tunnel end?* She wanted to ask Matt, as they could not go on like this forever. *Two breaths are not enough for this long distance!* The exertion of the swim alone sucked up every bit of precious oxygen.

A wave of cold current moved swiftly beneath her. *....there it is again.* She swallowed a scream of alarm; if she opened her mouth she would suck in water and that would be the end. Matt motioned to stay still and they clung again to the wall with one hand, their fingers gripping whatever projection of rock they could feel, and waited. The air share was much more difficult considering the adrenaline rush of terror, and the task of keeping legs still while grasping rock. They had to stay close so they could hand the mask between them. When they no longer sensed Snapper near, Matt handed Pattie the mask, pulling her to his side as they continued the swim.

When again she felt a surge of current beneath her, panic rose. The tunnel seemed endless, her lungs were bursting, and Snapper was close again. *Coward*! She fought back her fear with every inch of her oxygen-starved body, but the negative began to overtake the positive... *It's over.....* She wanted to cry, to scream, to push Matt away and be done with it!

Just in that detrimental moment, as if a gift from the gods, the river became shallower and their heads peeked above the surface. Pattie inhaled loudly, gasping at the precious air. "My God, he's in here! What do we do?"

An aggressive "thump' tossed them a foot into the air space. Patti's arm scraped against the cavern ceiling, and she dropped again into the green water, striking Matt. Beneath the surface, she instinctively opened her eyes, catching a quick flash of the massive, algae-covered carapace of Snapper as he sank out of view. Her heart pounded in extreme terror as she popped above the surface, thankful to see that Snapper had not carried Matt away. "What do we do? Where can we go! Hurry!"

Matt's dive light was a godsend. He tread a circle, shining the light against the craggy walls of their prison and there, a few feet away, was the smaller cave he and Steve had noticed on the first dive. "Quick! We're at the split!" He held the light on the smaller cave entrance and they swam—flew!—to its entrance. While Matt kept watch for Snapper, he motioned Patti to enter. She did not hesitate, and was grateful for the two or so feet of air space. Certainly they would be dead by now had the waters not become shallower. Air share would have been futile in their escape.

The smaller tunnel was at such an angle against the wall of the split in the main tunnel that Snapper, should he return, could not position his immense body to look inside for his prey without ramming his carapace against the wall of the cavern; the tunnel was much too small for him to follow.

When their fins touched the rocky floor, they stood. The cavern floor, in this smaller cave, had obviously elevated significantly.

"Oh, my God, my God!" Patti cried, holding out her hands to witness their severe trembling as she stood waist high in the water. She was suddenly cold, too; cold and terrified. Her shirt clung to her skin, feeling like a layer of ice. She could not stop the shivers that racked her body. Matt moved toward her, removing his equipment. When the last bit of gear was safely deposited in the shallows, he wrapped his arms around her shivering body, pulling her to him. " We have to warm you up, and *now*." She did not resist.

Once the shivering slowed, they tread further into the opening. He set the dive equipment on the ground, where they sat to rest. The limestone flooring was little protection to Patti's behind, covered only by the thin layer of her panties.

"Some scientist I am," she said. "I'm terrified, and I'm ashamed that I'm terrified"

"Why? Do you think that thing doesn't scare the wits out of me, too?"

"Do you think Steve and Kim made it?"

He looked her in the eye, "I don't know, but let's try and think positive."

"He could have easily killed us, you know."

"Yep."

"I don't understand why he didn't."

"I doubt it was the kindness of his heart," Matt replied.

"Unless…" she hated to think it. "Unless he had a different target."

"Let me know when you're ready to go." he said, ignoring her cryptic comment.

"We're not going back in in there, are we?

"We're going to explore this cave, and see where it goes. Maybe we'll get lucky."

* * *

Luck took its sweet time. The cave narrowed and expanded. At times, Matt could barely squeeze between the walls, and neither exited each narrow crevices without a new scratch or cut. Blood ran, trickling down legs and arms, but choices were nil; there was only one choice, and that was to continue. When the dive light began to flicker off and on, Matt shut it off.

"Stay close," he said.

They felt their way in the pitch black, bumping and groping through the dark and fickle tunnel. *Darker than dark,* she thought. First it was fear of Snapper. Now, it was fear of darkness. Matt had left his dive equipment back in the larger section. What if they ran into a deep section of river again? Would they have to retrace their steps through the horrid tunnel to retrieve it?

Forever passed before Matt stopped dead in his tracks.

"What?" She asked. "What's wrong?"

"Do you smell it?"

"What?" She sniffed the air, but her nostrils were sensitized to the atmosphere of the cavern and tunnel. "I smell nothing but this damned place," she answered. Reaching out, her hand found his muscled bicep. It was a relief to know someone was there.

"Never mind," he said. "Maybe it's a figment of my imagination," and they moved forward.

Soon, they sensed they were in a higher and wider section of the labyrinth. Matt flicked on the dive light. "This looks familiar, doesn't it?"

Patti followed the beam of light as it bounced off the magnificent stalactites and stalagmites of the Great Way. "Oh, no, we're back!" She plopped to the floor. She was tired, frightened, hungry, thirsty, and totally worn out. She wanted to scream, to cry—to kill Buzz. Anything to relieve this stressful terror!

Matt flashed the flickering light to follow the cavern river in the direction from which it flowed. "We haven't looked that way. Come on, maybe there's a way out, he said, holding out a helping hand.

This area continued as splendorous as the Great Way. Stalactites hung suspended from the high ceiling in an array of sizes and shapes that swirled and plunged artistically in mass presentation above the river, which now ran slowly as they walked.

"Look!" Matt said. "There seems to be a very faint light ahead."

"Oh, please let it be!" Patti whispered, anxious now to speed ahead and discover from where the light came. But when Matt's foot struck an object, they stopped. He singled it out with the light.

"I was hoping to spare you this. Steve and I discovered the missing divers when we first entered the cavern."

Patti gasped at the sight. A hand shot to her mouth to stifle a scream; his foot had found a severed arm. Scattered over the bumpy, craggy floor were body parts: feet, arms, the foot, part of a head, a torso, broken fleshy ribs with organs spilling out onto the limestone. She wanted to vomit.

"*River Ra*...Oh no, Gus!" she said, having read the few remaining letters on the torn and bloody fragment of shirt.

"Who?"

"It isn't just the divers, it's poor Gus! Just a nice old timer who ran a little charter fishing business."

In this state of horror she did not immediately register Snapper's stench, but when she did realize that he was in proximity, her hackles rose. "He's back! Quick, to the crevice again. He's coming!" she whispered.

"Maybe we should just continue this way, to the light." The dive light flickered, and Matt gave it a shake. It was now that they needed light more than ever!

"We don't know what's down there, and if that light goes, we're dead." Patti argued.

They backtracked to the Great Way and he shined the now erratic light across the expanse in search of the narrow crevice that had previously saved the four of them from Snapper's jaws. "There," he said. "Let's go."

They set out, but when Matt stopped at the river entrance where they had first begun their swim, Snapper's stench permeated the air. Mesmerized, as if not wanting to believe their bad luck, they stood staring into the dismal darkness, watching, waiting, until the light flickered upon Snapper's massive form, the dark eyes flinching against the strobe, a strobe that played tricks on their eyes, but none so cruel as the reality of the beast coming toward them; nearer, and nearer, flickering in and out of the failing dive light, his beady eyes forward, his lethal claws lifting, submerging as he neared.

They waited too long, for Snapper quickened his pace leaving no time to reach the crevice. "Back the way we came!" Matt yelled, propelling Pattie toward the narrow dark tunnel from which they had emerged before their encounter with the body parts. It was a macabre scene as they raced across the damp and stony cavern floor, dodging the stalactites and stalagmites visible only in the flicker of the failing dive light.

In one darkened moment Patti slammed against a stalagmite, falling to her knees. "Matt!" she screamed, certain that she had cracked a kneecap, for pain as sharp as a knife shot up her thigh to her hip. But there was no time to ponder her injury, for surely the beast was a breath away! The light blessedly flashed a moment on her fallen form as Matt returned to lift her quickly from the ground. Again, they headed for the passage, she limping in pain while the beast quickly approached, snapping his mighty jaws as he crashed through the smaller pillars and spikes of the cavern. These fell heavily to the ground, rolling and thumping against one another as Snapper unrelentingly followed the scent of his prey.

Once inside the passage they stood in darkness, gasping for air; Snapper could not follow them here as the entrance was too small for his massive form. Yet, the now dim dive light shone a moment on his horrid head, which barely fit into the opening. He snapped his beak and blasted foul air as he hissed his displeasure, filling the passage with the putrid smell of rotting plant and water life, the foul odor of death.

CHAPTER TWENTY-THREE

Buzz paced the kitchen floor. There was no way out; the police had come and they would be back. This rotten end was his payment for a lifetime of misery, a lifetime of caring for the man who hated him—accused him of killing the woman he loved. Well, hell, he had loved her too; she was his mother. She was all goodness and comfort. It was Snapper who had killed her, not him. It was his father who had killed her for raising the beast in the first place.

As the clock ticked away the moments, he became more and more agitated. The minutes passed as his shoes beat a rhythm on the wooden floor. He stopped to rest himself by the kitchen sink, leaning against the counter with strong arms braced by large hand, hands that told the tale of a hard-working outdoorsman, a man strong from his life in the diminishing woods of his homeland. *I'll finish it,* he thought. *There is nothing left.*

"That you, Buzz? Ain't it suppertime?" Elmer scooched a notch up against his sorry pillows as Buzz entered his room. "Where's supper, boy?"

Buzz smiled. "You're the supper today, old man."

"Eh?"

Buzz flung the sheets away from Elmer. "I said you're the supper today."

"I don't know what the hell you're talkin' about."

"You'll find out soon enough." Buzz leaned down and scooped his father into his arms.

"What'r'you doin'? Put me down. You gone crazy?"

"I told you," Buzz said as he carried Elmer down the stairs, "*You* are the supper tonight. I'm done with you. I'm done with your whining, pissing, shitting. I'm done with caring for you. You didn't care for me all these years. You done nothin' but torture me—blame me for Ma's death. Well now I'm gettin' rid of you." He laughed.

"Put me down, Buzz! You gone crazy, that's what. Put me down, *now*."

"I'm puttin' you down alright—down there, that's where!" He set Elmer on a chair at the table and opened the trap door.

"What'r'you doin' Buzz? You can't put me down there. Snapper's down there. Cut it out, it ain't funny!"

Buzz grabbed a flashlight, lifted Elmer like a rag doll, and flung him over his shoulder; the old man was light as a feather. Elmer attempted to pound Buzz on his back, but he was frail, weak, and helpless and his fists fell lightly on upon Buzz.

Carefully, Buzz flipped the switch to light the stairway. When he reached the bottom, he turned the flashlight on and scanned the area beyond the safety bars. Seeing that Snapper was not there, he wove through the stalactites and stalagmites caring not that he banged his father's head against a few as he went along, once breaking the tip of one, sending it rolling across the damp floor.

"Buzz…" his father's voice was weakened by his position on Buzz's shoulder. "Stop…this…now…." His voice was but a whisper as Buzz followed the flashlight into the Great Hall. Once into the massive cavern, he lay his father on the cavern floor.

"Your reward, you son of a bitch," he said. "May you rot in hell." He turned, and then stopped. "Oh, I almost forgot…Snapper!" he yelled. "It's suppertime!" His voice ricocheted against the dark, wet cavern walls as he left his father whimpering on the ground. Then, following the beam of the flashlight through the passage, through the steel bars, the stalagmites and stalactites, up the stairs into the kitchen, he switched off the light and slammed the trap door shut.

* * *

They had not moved since escaping Snapper. Instead, each took a seat against the damp, rocky wall, exhausted. Her knee throbbed with pain as they sat in gloomy silence beside one another.

"I'm sorry about Ted," Matt said after a while.

"I know. This is such a nightmare that I haven't even had time to adjust to his being gone—to the wonderful life we had planned—stolen away by a gruesome freak of nature. God, it was a horrible way to die and...and...and we'll probably go the same way."

"Nonsense. Don't even think it because I won't let it happen."

"And just how will we avoid it? We can't get into Buzz's house, and we can't get out through the river. Now I've hurt my knee, too. This just doesn't get any better."

"Listen," he said, reaching out in the pitch blackness to find her hand. "I won't let it happen, I promise."

"Don't make promises you can't keep," she said, removing her hand from his touch.

Again, they sat listening to the constant drip of the stalactites until a very faint light flooded the passage floor, and then the sound of voices.

"Wha...?"

"Shhh," Matt said. "Listen."

"It's Buzz, isn't it?" Patti whispered.

"I think so...there's someone else...I hear another voice."

Shortly, the light, already barely perceivable, disappeared.

"Buzz brought someone down."

"I know," Matt replied. "I'm going to go look. You stay here."

"No way. I'm coming with you."

"You're hurt."

"I won't sit here in the dark by myself."

Snapper had vanished, but they could not be certain as to *where* he had vanished. Perhaps an hour had passed since the threatening hissing had stopped and the signature claws breaking against the rocky floor had diminished into the depths of the cavern taking the stench of death with him.

Matt flipped on the dive light, tapping it, hoping there was a shred of battery power left. The light sputtered as they moved forward, relaying choppy glimpses of the mess the beast had made as he crashed through the natural barriers of the cavern in his effort to reach his prey.

"Hello?" Matt said in a low voice that whispered in echo around the massive walls.

"Huh?" was the reply. "Is someone down here?"

"Yes, we're trying to find you."

"Hurry!" said the old man, desperation in his voice. "Hurry, before Snapper comes!"

"Talk quietly so we can follow the sound of your voice." Matt said. "We don't want Snapper to come back, either."

Patti placed a hand on Matt's back to avoid separation as they stepped gingerly through the dark tomb, she, limping with pain. The old man continued to call out to his rescuers in a quiet, methodical way; and, finally, with the dive light dimming even more, they came across the skeletal figure of a shrunken clump of a man in pajamas, as he cowered against the cold wall of the Great Way.

"Thank God," Elmer said. "I don't know what's got into Buzz. Why'd he leave me here? I ain't forgiving him for this."

"Let's get you up and into the tunnel," Matt said. "Are you Buzz's father?"

"I am," Elmer grunted painfully as Matt lifted him to his feet.

"I can't stand on my own!" the old man said while fruitlessly trying to secure a grip on Matt's skin-tight wetsuit. "What you got on, boy, a slippery noodle?"

"A dive suit," Matt replied, and slung the frail man over his shoulder. He handed Patti the light, and she limped ahead, leading them. They were nearly to the passage entrance when she stopped dead; the stench of the beast was overpowering. There was no need for words, for blocking the tunnel entrance was the immense body of Snapper.

"Don't panic," Matt whispered.

"I *am* panicked," Patti replied as they stepped backward.

"What's goin' on?" Elmer mumbled breathlessly, as he had little air and no view of the beast from his awkward position over Matt's shoulder.

"It's Snapper. He's waiting for us," Matt whispered. "Be quiet."

Without warning, Snapper sprang as if he'd been shot from a cannon. "Hit the deck!" Matt yelled, breaking the 'whisper' rule, and they did—just in time. The old man wailed as he flopped onto the hard floor next to Matt, but gentleness had not been an option. The broken stalagmites and stalactites spun and rolled while Snappers' feet scrambled over them, but the intruders were safe; Snapper had straddled the trio as they lay in the space between the beast and the floor! The dive light, which had been fading rapidly, still shed enough of a glow to outline the opening of the passage. They wasted no time. Like scurrying mice, Patti and Matt each grasped a handful of Elmer's pajamas and dragged him like a sack of flour to safety.

Snapper again, having returned to the passage, thrust his giant head toward the opening, hissing his complaint, his beak snapping in rapid succession, razor sharp and strong as steel.

* * *

"It's not over yet," Matt said after the bruised, exhausted trio recuperated from their chilling experience and Snapper had grown tired of his antics. "I can make it through this tunnel and back to the river, I know I can. The dive equipment is there, and I can make a swim for it. If Snapper stays here, I have a great chance of getting out and getting help."

"He's a sneaky devil," she replied. What if he's waiting for you?"

"You're going to entertain him while I'm gone."

"Oh. Well, I always wanted to entertain a freakin' man-eating giant turtle that should never have weighed more than a couple hundred pounds at best." This she said flatly, staring into the pitch blackness of her surroundings. Physical and mental exhaustion reigned. She needed food for fuel, water for hydration. She needed a flashlight…she needed a better attitude…she needed to be free of this dark prison. She needed courage!

"How's the patient?" Matt attempted to turn on the dive light, but was rewarded with only a weak stream of light that quickly faded back into the blackness.

"Mr. Abbot?" Patti felt to her right where an occasional rumbling breath, as weak as the dive light, added to the unfriendly atmosphere. Her hand rested on a bony arm. "Mr. Abbot?" she inquired, once more to no reply. Her hand traveled to his throat, then to his head, which felt no more than a skull with skin. "He's very clammy."

"I'm leaving now. We need help, for us *and* for him."

"You have to wonder why Buzz would turn an old man out to such a fate as being eaten by a monster."

"Buzz is apparently a monster himself."

"I hope Kim and Steve made it."

"Me too."

She felt Matt's hand on her hair, and then her arm. "Be calm," he said. "Snapper is still out there. Sure smells like it, anyway."

"Good luck," she replied, her spirits sliding into a darker pit than the cavern. "Be careful. If I hear him move, I'll get his attention."

She was now bone weary, terrified, in pain, and practically alone in this nightmare. She was also ashamed; she was not her positive self. All her training—her experiences diving with creatures that could have easily killed her, her excitement over new discoveries—had absolutely not prepared her for the coward she had become. She was embarrassed and ashamed.

Mr. Abbot was asleep— or unconscious— and she wasn't sure how long he could hold on considering his physical condition. His mental state was unknown. The drip, drip, drip of the stalagmites and Mr. Abbot's erratic breathing were her only companions, except for the horrid freak of nature that reeked of putrid death; the creature that surely was out there in the greater cavern waiting....

* * *

She jerked awake—not remembering falling asleep—and reached to her eyes. *Are they open?* The darkness was more than she could imagine; she was blinded by it. Something had woken her. Her stomach? Her knee? Her bladder? She needed to pee, but was afraid to move for fear of losing her place and not being able to find Mr. Abbot again. *Silly...he's snoring...isn't he?* She listened, but could not zone in on any sounds from the old guy. *Is he dead?*

She was cold, as all she wore were her panties and tee shirt. Shivering, she crawled on all fours, her hurt knee shooting knives of pain with every move, but all the while hoping the direction in which she crawled was directly across from Mr. Abbot. When her head bumped against a rocky protrusion, she stopped to relieve herself. Now, to return, but how? How could she become disoriented so quickly? Listening for any sound from Mr. Abbot took all concentration, but she could not filter out the *drip, drip, drip* of the stalagmites. She cursed them; she promised herself she would never again enter a cavern, as she was sure the *drip, drip, drip* of the spheres that hung dramatically from the high ceiling above would haunt her forever. The dripping overcame her senses, becoming louder and louder until she wanted to scream. She muffled her ears with her hands, scrunched her face and wanted to end this nightmare!

Had she? Had she screamed? She must have, for now she heard and smelled Snapper's breath. *I woke him! Where is he?* Frantically, she turned her head in all directions. It was a futile act, for all was black. Snapper hissed, his beak snapped sharply; and with rising terror, Patti realized she had no idea in which direction to crawl. Hell was not fire and brimstone, it was here in the bowels of the earth, blinded by darkness.

CHAPTER TWENTY-FOUR

Matt squeezed through the last narrow slot of limestone walls before reaching the opening of the smaller tunnel that connected to the river. *Not far to go,* he thought, standing quietly in the chest high water listening for any sound of the beast. He was worried about Patti; she was hurt, scared, tired, hungry and thirsty. He was the same, but now he had a chance at freedom and would be able to get help for her and Mr. Abbot, not to mention coming up with a way to kill Snapper.

He had found and donned the dive equipment, and not hearing any sounds other than the natural splash of water lapping against the cavern walls, he stepped into the river and swam quickly toward the barred opening, grateful that he didn't need the dive equipment for this last leg.

The swim went smoothly and without danger. Once free from the cave, he climbed ashore and began the trek to home base in hopes that it was *still* home base. Perhaps Kim and Steve would have made it and had alerted another recovery team?

* * *

"Matt!" Sheriff Dave was the first to witness him breaking through the brush.

"Thank God you're still here," Matt said. "We need help right away."

"Wait…wait. First, what's going on? We have divers up and down this river searching for people, you and the other diver and Patti and her partner, Kim…."

"Right," said Chet, the reporter, who wasted no time approaching the men. He turned on a mini-recorder and held it by Matt's face. "What's the story so far?"

Matt waved away the recorder. "I don't have time for this. Patti is in danger, and so is Buzz's father. Have Kim and my diver returned?"

"Not to my knowledge," Sheriff Dave replied.

"Damn," Matt whispered. "Buzz has gone nuts. He's killed a man, injured Kim and dumped his own father in the cavern to be killed by Snapper."

"Snapper?" Both Sheriff Dave and the reporter said this in unison.

"It's the name of the beast."

"Beast?" Chet's eyes grew large, and he took a step backward. "What kind of a beast?"

Matt unzipped his dive suit. "A beast that can tear you in two with one snap of his jaws."

"My God," Chet whispered.

"I need water, Sheriff. Do you mind?"

"Sure thing," Dave called out to a deputy to retrieve a bottle.

"Listen," Matt said, as he peeled out of the dive suit which was now shredded at the knees and elbows from the rough walls and floor of the cavern. Raw and bleeding flesh were now exposed to air, leaving Dave to grimace at the sight. "We need to get the cops to Buzz's cabin right away. We have to get Patti and Abbot out of there before the beast gets them. Buzz has a rifle and isn't slow about using it, either. For Snapper, we need weapons—and big ones."

"I'm on it," Dave said. "I'll get men over to the cabin right away."

"I'm going with you," Chet said, but was ignored, as the team on the river bank now hustled like a pack of rats.

* * *

Once the Sheriff's car pulled up to Buzz's cabin, the yard filled quickly with uniformed police, most kneeling behind their open car doors, guns drawn. Matt and Chet were signaled to step behind the patrol car, which they did. Soon, a swat team arrived, and six heavily armed men filed out of their van, moving the uniformed police further away from the cabin. Three men were dispersed to cover the sides and back of the cabin through opposite sides of the woods. Two remained with a powerfully built team member who stood with a microphone behind the open door of the van.

"Buzz Abbot, surrender your weapons. You are surrounded."

Buzz did not respond. As there was not a cell signal in this particular area, a phone call from Buzz to the swat team would not occur. All was quiet as they waited. After several minutes, the man took the mic up again. "Buzz Abbot, you are surrounded. Free your hostages and surrender your weapons, *now*."

This time the response was breaking glass and a rifle shot causing every person in the yard to hit the ground. No one was hurt, and no shots were fired in return. The swat team communicated continuously with one another through mics and headphones, though Matt could not hear a word of what transpired. He was anxious…anxious for Patti and Mr. Abbot stuck in the dark dungeon of the cavern with Snapper. He was anxious for co-diver, Steve, and for Kim. His field was recovery; and so far, he had not been successful.

When the swat member with the mic attempted once more for a response from Buzz, all was silent. Uniformed police replaced the swat team members, whose positions were the sides and back of the cabin, while the swat team regrouped and kicked in Buzz's front door, entering with their weapons drawn.

After a few minute they returned, perplexed. "Nobody's in there," the powerfully built, heavily suited team captain reported to Sheriff Dave.

"Wait," Matt said, approaching the man. "I know where he is. There's a trap door in that house, and he must have escaped through it."

"And who are you?"

"Matt, Search and Rescue. I'm the one who escaped from the cavern. And who are you?"

"John, team captain. Where in the house is this trap door?"

"I'm not sure, but I can help you look."

"Let's go," John said, "but stay behind me."

With weapons ready to fire, the men again entered through the kitchen.

"Listen," Matt said, halting the group. "The beast is below us somewhere, as well as the hostages. It's dangerous, and your weapons may not do the job."

"Just find the door," the captain replied.

Matt perused the kitchen, overcrowded with the heavily armed swat team. The captain sent the team once more into the other rooms, which were very few: a living room, two bedrooms, and a small bathroom.

It wasn't difficult for Matt to spot the strange way the floor slanted toward a single spot in the room. "Look how the floor dips there, under the table." Matt bent at the waist, then dropped to his knees, leaning his torso beneath the table top. "Pretty obvious, wouldn't you say?" He pointed to the two finger holes on the trap door, and the slide lock.

The captain flushed, apparently embarrassed at the insinuation that his team had missed an important clue on their first search. He spoke into the small mike that sat at the side of a cheek, calling the rest of the team to return to the kitchen.

"Push the table aside," Matt said, and three team members lifted the table to expose the trap door. The captain knelt beside Matt, watching, as he slid the lock to the side, then stuck his fingers through the holes and lifted.

"Better lean back. That bastard has a rifle." Matt said, as the dank smell of earth and moisture wafted upward into the small space of the kitchen. Light filtered down a wooden stairway, and for a few moments, both men leaned backward, should Buzz be standing with his rifle at the bottom of the stairs.

The captain retrieved a slim flashlight from his uniform and aimed it down the stairway, circling the perimeters that were visible from their position. "Release the hostages and turn yourself in," the captain yelled through the opening and then motioned all to stand back should there be a response.

Nothing.

They waited, and still nothing.

Matt recalled that Buzz had once turned on a light in the cavern. He reached into the opening and felt the underside of the floor wondering if Buzz was taking aim at that very moment at his figure outlined by the light filtering through the kitchen window.

"I know there's a switch here," he said, and lay on his stomach in order to extend his arm further into the opening. "Damn," he said in frustration, finding nothing. Then, something tickled his arm, and he reached for it. A string! One pull, and light flooded the stairway, exposing a small section of the cavern below. Hopefully, there was no threat from Buzz in this vicinity—or from the beast.

"Stay here," the captain ordered.

"I will not," Matt replied. My job is to save the people down there, and that's exactly what I'm going to do. If that beast is there, you'll have your hands full."

The captain begrudgingly agreed, and Matt was ordered to enter the cavern last in the line. Once down, he noticed that the swat team had spread out on the safe side of the protection bars, weapons drawn and ready to shoot whatever came their way first, Buzz or his beast.

"I have to go through that passage." Matt indicated the direction of the curved tunnel off to the right, on the other side of the safety bars. "Can you spare another one of those lights?"

"No need. We're coming with you."

"Look," Matt replied, growing weary of Captain John's reluctance to let him participate. "I realize I'm not a member of the team, but I have plenty of experience dealing with people in trouble. I'm a recovery diver by occupation, and an ex-marine, so quit pushing me aside. You don't know this beast, and I do. You need my help."

John shifted in place. "Okay, buddy. Sorry. We just don't want anyone getting in our way, or getting hurt because of our tactics. Hey, Joe!" The captain called to one of the swat team. "Send a light this way."

With light in hand, Matt led the way through the curved tunnel. Once through the passage, they entered into the Great Way. A few whispered exclamations of surprise from the swat team reached his ears, as the flashlights scoured over the magnificent splendor of the cavern.

"Will you look at this place!" a member exclaimed while beaming his own flashlight at the magnificent and artistic spheres that hung in macabre display.

"You can smell the beast before he shows his ugly face," Matt informed the team. "He'll knock you over with his stink, but he doesn't seem to be here at the moment. "Patti!" he called, heading toward the location of the smaller tunnel on the opposite side of the cavern. "We're here—Patti!"

The others followed behind, shining their lights in all directions, attuned to a monster in their midst. Halfway across the expanse, the first scent of Snapper's pungent odor drifted up Matt's nostrils. So concentrated was he on finding Patti that he missed the first warning. Snapper's preemptive warning did not register until a second and stronger odor drifted into the cavern.

Matt stopped the group. "He's here!" he whispered, in a voice that did not hide alarm.

"Where?" the captain asked.

"Don't know."

The team immediately formed a small circle, side by side, facing outward. Matt cut in to stand with them. In this way, they were able to peruse the entire cavern at once.

"I see nothing," one man said, his light bouncing off craggy walls.

"Me either," said another.

"Wait…" Matt shined his light down the passage that led to the main river. "He's coming from there!" Indeed, his light had reflected movement in the distance.

At seventy-five feet, Snapper appeared a strange object far into the black riverbed, barely visible in the stream of flashlights. At fifty feet, murmuring circled amongst the men, as Snapper's form was now taking shape. At thirty feet, alarm overcame the armed and heavily outfitted heroes of the swat team, for now the beast's algae mottled carapace was taking horrifying form. Snapper barreled forward, his mighty daggered claws splashing through the shallowing waters of the underground river, not flinching from the glaring light that outlined his horrid head and features.

"Wait...hold your fire...wait..." the captain said quietly, watching the monster approach.

"You'd better shoot now!" Matt yelled, ready to take off like a track star.

The cavern erupted into a theater of blazing flashes and deafening blasts as the weapons fired, resounding off the high ceiling and stony wall to stony wall of the Great Way. But the beast kept coming, hissing, while his great beak snapped against the barrage of ammunition.

From the flashes of light, Matt could see chips of carapace fly as shrapnel, but the barrage of artillery only seemed to spur the beast forward; he was not to be defeated in this fashion.

"Run!" Matt yelled, but the blasting of weapons drowned him out. His warning was unnecessary with Snapper nearly upon them.

Weapons ceased. The light from the stairway was nil at this location, just a faint glow seemingly a great distance away. Matt attempted to direct the men toward the narrow tunnel where Patti and Mr. Abbot should be waiting, but they scattered like rats into the darkness. His voice could not be heard over their yelling, as the men escaped into this unknown and dark territory.

Realizing his directions were in vain, Matt felt his way toward the tunnel, mindful of the clumps of spirals that could hamper his path. Sweat ran like a river from his scalp as he groped stalagmites, weaving between them like a blind man—which he nearly was, with only the flashlight to guide him!

Men stumbled and fell over the cavern's debris, yelling as broken pieces of spirals rolled and clunked at their disturbance; it was a madhouse; it was the blackest of nightmares. Then, as if the chaos were not enough, a piercing yell—scream!—resounded through the darkness. It was the ultimate scream of terror as one unfortunate hero had surely been pierced by Snapper's mighty beak.

CHAPTER TWENTY-FIVE

It took a moment for Patti to register the commotion; it was as if she had woken up in a war zone. But it *was* a war zone! Though terrified by the rude awakening of gunfire, men's voices—*frantic voices*—and one blood-curdling scream, she was ultimately relieved that she was no longer alone in this dark hell, that there was hope of recovery for herself and Mr. Abbot.

Sporadic flickers of light bounced off the walls of her prison, allowing her a quick view into her surroundings. In one such flicker, she witnessed Mr. Abbot slumped against the tunnel wall across from her position. *Dead?* She could not take the time to dwell on his condition; Snapper was out there. She could smell the stench of him, hear him—the sharp dagger claws scrambling across the limestone floor—the horrifying sound of his piercing beak snapping shut. Men were out there fighting for their lives, blinded by darkness.

"Matt!" she called over the cacophony of chaos in the Great Way, and was relieved to hear her name in return. Within moments she heard heavy breathing as he stumbled into the safety of the tunnel.

"Thank God you're here!" she said, reaching out, hoping to feel his presence. A quick flash of light brought his outline into view. He was on all fours now, crawling quickly toward her.

"What's happening out there?" she asked.

"Swat team, but they've scattered." The quick flash of light had now dispersed into the blackness of the cavern. She reached out again and felt his head, damp from exertion. She wanted to cry from relief, but the horror continued. It was not over yet.

"I don't know if Mr. Abbot is alive. He's across the way but we can't see him now."

"We'll have to worry about him later. I think one of the swat team got it, but the others…I just don't know."

After a while, nothing could be heard but Snapper's pacing. "He's looking for more people," Matt whispered. "The trap door is open, and if we can get to it, we're home free."

Patti shuddered. The thought of traversing the Great Way to the tunnel and into the safety area seemed a pipe dream at this point.

"We don't have much choice," Matt said, as if reading her mind. "There's no other way out now."

"Where's Buzz? Did you get him?"

"That's another thing. We think he's down here somewhere. The swat team had the place surrounded. We know he was in the cabin because he took a shot at us, but he's disappeared. He has to be down here."

"Great." *Can it get worse?*

* * *

When Snapper's pacing dissipated into silence, and his stench gone, Matt crawled to the tunnel entrance. "Hello out there!" he called "Don't come out. Just yell back so we know you're okay."

"Yo!" a man yelled, then another and another, until there were five replies, including John, the team captain.

"Names!" The captain yelled, after which each member called out their name. "Brandon?" the captain called, but there was no reply. "Crap," he said. "Matt, we need to get back to the kitchen!"

"I know. I can go ahead and let you know if the coast is clear."

"I'm coming with you," Captain John replied.

Patti grabbed for Matt's arm in the darkness. "Don't," she whispered. "Let them; they're the swat team."

"I know this cavern better than they do," he answered.

"Then I'm coming with you, too," she said.

"No, you stay here with Abbot."

"I'm coming with you," she said, and meant it. "We go together."

"Anybody still have a light out there?" Matt asked.

"I do." The captain replied.

Once Matt and Patti were hand in hand at the river entrance, they waited for the promised hint of another flashlight. Patti had limped to the opening, her knee shooting arrows of pain to her hip.

"You need to stay here," Matt said, realizing the extent of her injury.

"No way. I'm done waiting. I won't hold you back— promise."

The captain appeared several feet away, a haunting figure highlighted in one beam of light, the towering shadows of spires enveloping him. "You're not coming," he said, shining the light briefly on Patti.

"I am," she said, adamantly. "I won't stay here another minute."

"It's okay," Matt said. "She's with me."

"At your own risk," Captain John said, and searched the crags and corners of the Great Way with the light.

"He's not here. I can't smell him," Matt said. "Let's go."

They tread single file across the expanse of the cavern, the captain in front with his light, then Patti, and Matt taking up the rear. "There's no signal down here," the captain said. "We need to call in another team; this creature is bigger than we thought, so we're going to need some heavy weaponry."

Olfactory senses were never as important as they were now. Patti and Matt continuously sniffed the dank air for any hint of Snapper as they made their way through the curved passage toward the safety zone. As they approached the sanctuary, the one light bulb from the stairway brightened their path. When nearly around the last curve of the passage way, it hit them, the smell of mud and algae, the smell of rotting fish, the smell of death, *the smell of Snapper.*

He's waiting.... Patti's shame at cowardice surfaced. She snuffed the trembling of her body, straightened her shoulders, and steadied her voice. "He's here," she said, fighting— with every muscle in her body— the urge to run.

"Steady," Matt whispered.

They couldn't see Snapper, so they listened for movement. Nothing. They crept quietly until they reached the safety of the bars. Once in the safety zone, they searched every darkened corner of the chamber with their eyes, looking for the beast.

Click.

A gun? "Did you hear that?" Patti whispered.

"Sounded like a gun safety taken off," Matt whispered.

"Welcome back!" Buzz appeared from the darkness beneath the stairwell. "So glad to see you!" He pointed a 30-30 rifle directly at the trio. "Where are the other brave folks? I saw y'all come down into this hell-hole, you know. We can have a real party watching Snapper eat his dinner…or *dinners,* I should say. If there's one thing I love, it's watching Snapper eat."

"You're crazy, Buzz," Matt said. "There are cops everywhere. You can't get away."

"Ha! Cops up there, and a swat team hiding like cowards in there," he said, nodding toward the curved passage. "My only problem at the moment is getting rid of you folks. I'll worry about the brave swat team later."

"You won't get out of here alive," the captain said. "Hand over your weapon."

"I think it's *you* who won't get out of here alive, Mr. Swat Team. I plan on getting out of here with all my pieces intact."

"You're a fool," Patti said.

"Say that again, bitch."

"You're just like that creature out there, a beast! What kind of man leaves his own father to be killed by a monster?"

"Get over here," Buzz ordered. Patti did not move. "Get over here!" he yelled again. "I'll blow your friend's brains out if you don't start movin'!"

With trepidation, she stepped forward until Matt told her to stop.

Buzz pointed the rifle directly at Matt. "You don't believe me? I have nothing to lose, so I don't mind blowing you away. Don't matter to me."

Patti was midway between Matt and Buzz and in a conundrum. *Move forward or not? Is he bluffing?* She opted to move forward and did, ever mindful of the jabbing pain from her injured kneecap. When she was close enough, Buzz reached out and yanked her to him in a choke hold. She gagged as he cinched her to his chest. Instinctively, she reached her hands up, gripping his powerful forearm in an attempt to release the death hold, but it was a futile gesture.

Buzz inched his way to the safety rails dragging the struggling Patti. "Snapper!" he yelled. "Got dinner!" Then, "You gotta see him chomp this little lady up. It's quite the show."

"You're insane," Captain, John, said. "Let her go; you're in trouble enough. There's a whole army of...." The captain flew backward, struck by a bullet. Patti shrieked in horror as a fountain of blood sprang from his forehead. Captain John fell to the floor in a crumpled heap, unmoving, dead to all that had transpired and would transpire in this theater of death.

Snapper, from a dark and hidden corner of the chamber, burst forward with such speed and agility, that even Patti, suffering the chokehold in Buzz's grip— and the murder she had just witnessed— eyed the beast barreling toward them. Her eyes grew large with terror. *I can't go this way!*

Buzz appeared to be confused at the direction of Snapper's sudden appearance. In the brief moment that Buzz's attention was diverted from Matt to Snapper, Matt took advantage. He lunged into Buzz and freed Patti, flinging her away from her assailant. He felt for the rifle and wrestled it out of Buzz's grip, pinning him against a metal bar.

Buzz fought like a wild man—fists, knees and head—all packed into one solid body of muscle, and all punching, kicking and striking in nonstop fury. He smacked his head hard against Matts', sending him flying onto the hard floor. It was a timely move as both men were removed from the spot where Snapper had just stopped short to bang his carapace against the metal bars.

Matt rose and kicked the rifle away just as Buzz had bent to retrieve it, sending it clanging against the steel bars where it rested out of reach. In his own fury, Snapper had managed to bow two of the bars. Now his head stretched to outlandish lengths between them as his massive jaws snapped repeatedly in an attempt to catch hold of either man.

Patti rushed to the captain's aid and saw that he was dead. She dragged him further away from Snapper, as he had fallen within reach of the monster's snapping jaws. At least she would save him the offense of ending his life as turtle food. He would receive a hero's burial. Then, seeing that it was a race between the men for the rifle, she ran toward the hideous head of the beast. "This way!" she yelled, waving her arms frantically in an attempt to turn his attention from them. "Here, this way!"

Snapper eyed her with one dark prehistoric glance and snatched his head from the bowed bars. She watched in rising terror as he approached. To be so near the beast was unthinkable! Without hesitation the creature began to ram his armored body repeatedly into the steel safety bars with such horrific force that they began to bend. Bars that held securely in place for decades, now bent at sharp angles as the algae mottled carapace rammed time and time again. He slammed into the steel like a battering ram until his head again protruded into the safety zone. With jaws snapping ferociously, he narrowly missed piercing Patti. She jumped backward— and none too soon—as a clawed leg shot forward, narrowly missing her foot. Still, she continued to yell and wave, keeping his attention, unknowing of the outcome of the struggling men.

"It's not going to hold!" she yelled, hoping Matt heard her plight. "The bars are bending!" she screamed, and sure enough, Snapper, with one powerful thrust, popped the bars out of their cement holdings and sent them flying as if they'd sprung from a jack-in-the-box. Stalactites and stalagmites crashed to the floor as he injected himself into his new territory. He was now free to pursue his prey in the safety zone—but only for a short distance, as the ceiling was too low for him to advance forward. His frustration was apparent by his snapping and hissing, his foul breath permeating the airspace in thick blasts of putrid stench.

Matt did hear her, for now they were side by side backing further into the narrowing crevice. In a side glance, Patti witnessed Buzz collapsed on the cavern floor. "Where's the rifle?" she asked.

"Not sure," Matt replied, grabbing onto her hand. "We have to get to the stairway. It was chancy. Though Snapper could not fit his body into their tight area, his neck stretched to incredible lengths; they were not safe yet.

"Hey!" came a voice from the stairwell. What's going on down there? Was that a shot? We've lost contact."

"Stay up there, the beast is loose! We're coming up as soon as we can get there," Matt yelled. "We need big weapons here, so alert the others."

"Where's the swat team?"

"The captain is dead, and so is another man." Matt said. "Don't know about the others, they scattered. "Hurry up and get help. Call an ambulance while you're at it."

Buzz came to and sat, obviously orientating himself. "You sonofabitch," he yelled at Matt, focusing on the pair trapped by Snapper some distance away.

At the sound of his voice, Snapper turned his head to eye Buzz. He stared with beady black eyes at his caregiver. Buzz returned the stare and sat stone still. "Where's the rifle?" he asked, his voice now low and desperate.

"Lost," Matt answered. "Don't move."

"Don't!" Patti said, grabbing Matt's arm as he took steps toward Buzz.

Matt shook her hand away. "Can't let this happen," he said and ducked through the stalactites at the narrowest section of the cavern until he stood fifteen feet from Buzz, who still sat quietly, searching with fear-filled eyes for the lost weapon. Snapper crept step by step toward him, his great and horrid head lowered to meet Buzz's gaze.

The tension was so intense that Patti had forgotten to breathe. She inhaled loudly, which inadvertently seemed to wake Snapper from his trance. He opened his deadly beak and hissed a hiss that was nearly a howl. Buzz closed his eyes against the assault of fetid breath and jumped to his feet.

"This way!" Matt yelled, indicating the stairway, but Snapper had lunged his snakelike neck toward Buzz, who jumped backward, turned and ran toward the Great Way passage. Snapper was not about to lose his prey; he scrambled across the floor after him. Patti stared unbelievably as Matt leapt over broken stalagmites and ducked the spirals that hung from the upper ceiling as he followed suit. She screamed for him to stop, and he did— but only after the beast stopped suddenly.

First, she heard the scream of terror. Then, when Snapper turned, Buzz dangled in his beak by one leg. He beat frantically at his captor, at the air, at his beak, at anything in range, all the while his screams echoing through the chamber at ear-shattering decibels.

Snapper swung Buzz like a carnival ride. Patti covered her eyes against the horror for a moment, and when she opened them, Buzz was on the cavern floor—one leg missing—and dragging his body as he desperately clawed his way to the safety zone, which was safe no longer.

Matt ran to help him, but backed off when Snapper approached his wounded victim. Buzz's severed leg was visibly pinched between his powerful jaws.

"Oh, my God!" Patti yelled, watching Buzz's desperate crawl, blood pouring from his severed stump.

Matt seemed to be dancing and leaping in front of the giant beast. His attempts to grab ahold of Buzz's arms were fruitless as Snapper's focus was on Buzz, only. All hope for rescue was lost when the beast raised an enormous forefoot and slammed it downward, impaling Buzz with one mighty clawed foot.

Buzz screamed in pain as he was now skewered through the abdomen, attached to Snapper as an appendage; but he continued to reach out. "Save…me…." he said, stretching a weakening arm out to Matt, who now stood helplessly watching the scene play out.

Patti could see that it was hopeless. Under the one light of the chamber, blood ran a river. Snapper now chomped on and swallowed the severed leg. When he moved, Buzz moved with him, attached to his foot like an odd shoe. It appeared the creature was headed toward the dark corner from which he had come, when suddenly his neck stretched full length. He swung his head, smashing Matt in the gut, the force of which sent him flying toward the Great Way passage.

Patti screamed. She quickly glanced toward the open trap door, and then to Matt, who had hit the wall of the cavern and was slumped motionless against it.

She teetered a moment between escape and saving Matt. *Can't live with myself if I leave now*, she thought, and scurried through the debris of broken cavern spires toward the wall of the passage.

"Matt!" She ran toward his body and saw, with much relief, that he was now moving—and groaning.

"God, that thing has a wallop," he moaned.

She helped him to his feet and then noticed that Snapper had changed direction and was now staring at them through his dark and terrifying eyes. A quick look at Buzz's torn and mutilated body attached to the creature's foot convinced her he was dead. Snapper charged. It was a bizarre sight, as Buzz also charged forward with every step the beast took, impaled as he was on the creatures foreleg.

Words were not necessary; they were now blocked from their only escape route, the trap door. They literally ran, sheer fright setting the pain in Patti's knee to the back of her mind. Through the passage, with Snapper fast on their trail, they entered into the darkness of the Great Way. The beast had the advantage, as it appeared he was able to focus in the blackness, and they were not.

"The tunnel!" Matt said. At a lost for any sense of direction, they held hands and ran helter-skelter. Patti prayed they would make it, blinded now as they were with the darkness and fearful of running straight into the stalactites and stalagmites that protruded and descended at random. One fall could prove fatal, and she was determined that they would not end up like Buzz.

They couldn't be sure, but as they scrambled through the carnage of dropped weapons, and broken spires, the atmosphere changed, as they were forced to bend lower as they scurried.

"Is this it?" Patti asked.

"I can't tell, but I think we may be safe for now."

Snapper had stopped the chase, and all was quiet aside from the constant natural sounds of the cavern, and their heaving breaths from the exertion.

"Swat Team!" Matt yelled.

"Yo!" came a reply. "We're all together. Where's that thing?"

"He's in here. Stay where you are. Do you have a light?"

"Yes."

"Turn it on so I can see your location."

In a moment, a flashlight lit a beam to their location within the curtain of spires. Patti looked behind and caught the darkened curve of the passage opening in which Mr. Abbot had been left.

"Thanks!" Matt yelled, as the light came from a distance away in the direction of the pile of Gus's remains that he and Patti had discovered previously. "Okay, turn it off. Save the battery. We're not safe yet and may be in here for a while."

The light flicked off. "Where's the captain?"

"He's dead, shot. Buzz Abbot is dead, too."

Meanwhile, Patti had made her way in the direction of the tunnel. The pain in her knee had returned; but despite that, she felt her way into the tunnel by running her hands against the right side wall until her feet bumped an object. She bent, painfully, to touch the body of Mr. Abbot. He groaned.

"Matt! He's alive!"

"Keep talking so I can find you."

"He made a sound." She felt for his head and found that it was warm. "Mr. Abbot, can you hear me? We're here to help you."

"Buzz? That you?" the old man asked.

Matt shuffled into the tunnel following the sound of their voices and stopped when he bumped Patti with his foot.

"I'm Matt and this is Patti. You just hold on, buddy, and we're going to get you out of here and to a hospital."

"Where am I?" the old man asked.

"We're in a cavern below your house."

"Snapper!"

"Don't worry. You're safe."

Silence. "Buzz put me here. Don't know what's wrong with that boy. He needs a good thrashing."

"When we're out of here," Matt agreed, not telling him that his son was dead.

"I'm thirsty. You got water?"

"Can't get it, sorry. That beast is out there. We'll get it as soon as it's safe."

"That beast...Snapper. I should'a killed the thing way back when it killed my Jane. So horrible...so horrible the way she went...."

"Let's talk about that later," Patti piped in, sensing the man was on the verge of tears. She felt for his shoulder, bony thing that it was, and gave it a pat. "Later," she said. "Rest awhile."

"Let's move to the other side." Matt tapped her arm. "Come on."

They moved together, fearful of losing one another in the pitch of blackness, and sat, leaning against the damp stony wall.

Patti's head throbbed, along with her swollen knee. With the adrenaline dissipating, her body settled into an exhausted, yet restful state. She wanted to sleep and wake up in her bed. "I wonder if it's still daylight out there. It's impossible to keep track of time now."

"There has to be a way out," Matt said, ignoring her last words. "That man needs medical help and so do you."

Matt crawled to the opening. "Swat team!"

"Yo!"

"We need to get our heads together and figure a way out."

"What about upstairs? Do they know our predicament? We can't reach them."

"They do, but I don't know what they're doing about it."

"They'd better figure something out, and fast."

"In the meantime, we have to keep proactive or we'll die down here."

Snapper hissed, reminding them of his horrid presence.

"Damn! That thing is still there, just waiting for dinner—that being *us,*" one of the swat members remarked.

Soon splashing sounds reached their ears, first loudly and then grew quieter until none were heard at all. The stench of the beast was gone.

"He went into the river," Patti said, much relieved. "They like to be wet."

"That's one for our team." Matt said and then called across the expanse. "The beast has left us for a while!"

Within moments flashlights beamed in their direction and outlines of men advanced toward them. "We're coming to your side," a man said as he entered the tunnel. "It looks much cozier than ours. Who's that guy?" he asked, flashing the light onto Mr. Abbot, whose eyes resembled black pits in the recessed sockets of a bony skull. He sat slumped against the tunnel wall like a living skeleton, a few sprays of thin hair sprouting from his scalp.

"It's Buzz Abbot's father. Buzz left him here to be killed by the beast."

"No good son of Satan," Mr. Abbot mumbled.

"I'd have to agree with you on that, sir," the man replied. "I'm Bob, and this is what's left of the team: Mark, Sam and Phil.

"This is Miss Tripp." Bob shined the light on Patti, to the sound of a few whispers from behind.

"Just pretend it's a bathing suit." She felt very intimidated now that the troops were together. She had totally forgotten that her jeans were missing, and here she sat in bikini undies and a tee shirt!

"Keep your mind on the matter at hand," Matt ordered. Miss Tripp is a marine biologist and has been through hell. She's been trapped in this cave for quite a while and deserves a medal for her bravery."

"Yes, sir. Sorry ma'am," Bob said, and then whacked the nearest team member with his flashlight.

CHAPTER TWENTY-SIX

Two men stood guard as the others gathered the weapons and searched for flashlights amongst the debris littering the cavern floor. At Snapper's attack, weapons had flown helter-skelter in the men's escape from the beast, and now it was time to retrieve them for their escape to the trap door.

"I think he went down the river," Patti said, with some doubt. "Hopefully, he didn't go the other way." She shined a borrowed flashlight to the continuation of the river, which flowed past the site of Gus's remains. "We don't know where it leads."

"We don't need to know at this point, if we can just reach the trap door and get the hell out of here," Bob said. "Are we ready?" he yelled to the men in the shadows of his flashlight.

"Yep," came the reply, so the group of six walked across the Great Way, leaving Elmer behind with the promise to send aid when they reached the ambulance crew that, hopefully, would be waiting up top. He pleaded to come with them, but they simply could not risk the escape with a frail, old man.

"I feel awful leaving him there," Patti said, walking next to Matt.

"He should be moved by the professionals." Matt flashed a light down the river tunnel as they passed. "All clear," he said.

"I know, but he's old and afraid."

"hat's the point, he can't travel. Let's just get out of here first, and then take care of Abbot."

The group entered the passageway to the escape chamber and followed the faint beam of light from the one remaining light bulb, which had blessedly remained intact.

Just as they approached the curvature of the passage walls, Patti stopped. "Damn!" she whispered. "I think he's in there!"

"You're right," Matt said. "I can smell him."

"What now?"

"We can try to reach the door, but he's very fast."

"I'm game," piped one of the men, and then the others.

"We need to shoot that light out first." Matt said.

"He can focus in the dark," Pattie replied.

"Well, shit! Damn smart of him to wait for us here, wouldn't you say?" one of the team members piped in.

"He's crafty for sure," Patti agreed. "Maybe he can't focus fast, if we're quick enough once the light is out."

Once at the end of the passage, the grouped halted. "Put a beam on the staircase," Matt ordered. "Keep together single file, hold onto each other's shirts. When the light goes, move like lightning. He knows we're here, he just isn't charging yet. Maybe we have a chance if we keep ourselves calm."

"Phil, get the light," Bob ordered.

Bang, and it was done, total darkness. The trap door was open, but apparently it was nighttime as the door was only faintly outlined; but it was enough to spot the door in the otherwise pitch blackness.

"Go!" Matt said, leading the group. Patti held tight to his shirt and Bob held tightly to hers, and so on down the line.

Twenty feet from the door, the inevitable hiss alerted the group to Snapper's awareness. Just vaguely they could see his approach, slow, not fast as they had expected. He seemed to creep like a cat after prey, one foot, then the other, a mountainous mass of stinking algae over a rock-hard carapace.

They quickened their pace, anxious to reach the stairway before Snapper's cat-like approach changed to that of a raging bull.

The stairs! Matt had one foot on the stairs, when Snapper's demeanor changed dramatically. The force of his rotten breath, alone, nearly knocked them over.

"Shoot!" Bob yelled, and the three tail-end men did just that, sending a stream of bullets at the beast as the others scrambled.

But Snapper could not be stopped in this way. Though he did not fit completely beneath the lower canopy of ceiling at this end, his snake-like neck did. He stretched it like a rubber band, grabbing the last man in line and tossing him into the jagged teeth of stalactites.

Patti scrambled up the stairs behind Matt, fear choking all but the will to survive. Just as they reached the trap door, the stairway began to shudder and move. It creaked and moaned as Snapper, with his head, had torn it away from the opening!

Matt hung onto the doorframe for dear life and dangled there, as the entire flight of stairs, now unattached to the trapdoor, crashed to the floor below. Patti was thrust against a stalactite and dropped like a brick. The fall knocked the wind out of her, but at least she was alive, the staircase crashing just feet from her prone body.

"Matt!" she screamed. "Bob!" but her screams only intermingled with those of the men who had been in line behind her, as they scrambled for their lives.

Snapper raged, his great beak snapping, making contact, men hollering as they were impaled by beak or claw. It was a madhouse. Patti crawled into the furthest recess which would have been beneath and behind the staircase, were it still there. "Matt!" she called again. She cursed the blackness of the cave. She cursed the beast, and the cavern itself, for it had brought nothing but misery and death. *Hopeless!* She thought. *We can't escape; there's no way out now!* Her heart beat in rapid rhythm, sweat poured from her face and down her neck. *Are they all gone? Am I alone?*

"Help!" she screamed. Surely the police had not deserted them. Surely there were ambulances and more swat teams up above. Surely a plan was being worked to save them—*if there are any survivors*—surely they hadn't been abandoned! "Help!" she screamed again, and then nearly sobbed with relief when Matt answered her. She heard a scraping across the floor and imagined that Snapper had somehow reached a horrid, clawed foot toward her and would soon impale her—drag her like a shoe—as he had done to Buzz.

The scraping came closer, and she screamed.

"It's me, Matt."

This time, she did sob. "…the…the others?"

"I don't know," Matt said, pulling his body up beside hers and exhaling in exhaustion as he leaned against the cool damp wall.

All was quiet, except for Snapper, who could be seen as a giant shadow from their perspective. He shuffled around the chamber, perhaps cleaning up the carnage; they didn't know.

"Anyone okay out there?" Matt asked, but there was no reply.

"Why don't they help us?" she cried. "They know we're here, but they don't come!"

He took her hand. "They will come. They won't leave us here."

"Listen," Patti said, again overcoming a jab of guilt over her cowardice. "There's obviously another passage in the direction Snapper came from. The river probably runs through there and maybe his den is down there somewhere. Only one entrance is barred, but what about the other entrance? Maybe it opens out somewhere?"

"For all we know, this river could run for miles and miles underground." Matt said.

"I know, but maybe there's another way out. Maybe we should try and find it, *if* this is true."

"We'll need the flashlights. When he leaves, we'll see if we can find them."

They waited, and felt that Snapper was waiting, too— for *them*. When Snapper did shuffle away, he left by way of the old passageway, leaving the coast clear for them to explore the trail of the river.

"Come on. Let's look for flashlights and weapons."

"You're limping," Patti said, noticing the unevenness of his step.

"Just like you!" he answered, nudging her in the ribs. "I was dangling like a worm on a hook up there. Good turtle bait. I had to drop, but jammed my ankles."

"We're a mess," Patti said.

Once out in the open, the carnage was not seen because of the darkness of the chamber, but carnage was well felt when feet bumped an object. Fearing that she was nudging body parts, Patti only bent to retrieve a weapon, and then a flashlight that rolled when making contact with her feet.

Once a flashlight was in hand, the scene was grotesquely lit by random beams of light. Of the four men, one and one half were visible in the immediate area. Though her stomach was void of any food,

Patti's urge to vomit overtook her at the site of Bob's intestines trailing from his torso. She gagged and ran to the nearest wall. When she returned, the taste of bile still in her throat, she shined the light straight ahead, not wanting to see more of Snapper's handiwork.

"I can't..." she said. "It's awful!"

"Come on and bring that rifle." They both hooked their arms through assault weapon strap. He took her hand and weaved through the littered cavern floor, stepping over and around whatever reminder of carnage was visible. Matt stopped to pick up a spare ammo clip.

Having found the river, they discovered there was enough of a rocky path to walk upon, and they had flashlights to lead them. The river was wide enough for Snapper's immense carapace. The ceiling was high, and the side walls full of crags and crevices. After several minutes of walking in tense silence, they came to another chamber.

"Let's see what's here," Matt said, and they scanned the area with their lights. "Looks like a passage over there."

"This is huge," Patti said with wonder. "It's amazing what's beneath us when we're walking on land. This is a perfect haven for a creature as large as Snapper."

"As long as he can feed. Maybe there's another entrance that he uses. Otherwise, with the first entrance barred, he'd starve to death if us idiots weren't down here."

Patti shot a hand out to grasp his arm. "Oh, my God," she whispered. "There's light!"

Sure enough, in the distance, it was possible to make out another chamber, thanks to a light source they could not see from this angle.

"Let's go!" Patti led the way, hopeful now that there was the possibility of escape—*another way out.*

CHAPTER TWENTY-SEVEN

"**M**aybe fifty feet," Matt said, perusing the craggy hole in the cavern ceiling. The light from an awakening day filtered down into the cavern as a beam of hope; billions of golden sunlit particles lit the way of their escape to freedom.

"How the heck can we get up there?" Patti crossed her arms over her chest and stared at the light. Oh, how she wanted to be up there! Though they were able to hydrate themselves with river water, hunger was the enemy. In silent moments, with their attentions directed otherwise than the giant creature that pursued them, hunger raised its head. Patti's stomach growled and she felt nauseous as they stood highlighted in the one beam of daylight. They desperately needed free of this place. She silently cursed the police and all the others who were up there safe from Snapper, while she and Matt struggled to free themselves *without* their help. How many were dead? What happened to Kim and Steve? So many questions and no answers, as long as they were stuck in this hell hole.

"Look here," Matt said. He had removed himself to a wall in which a series of jutting rocks projected from base to top. "How are you at rock climbing? If we can get to the top, we're home free."

"Oh, boy." Patti thought of her throbbing knee and Matt's sore ankles—not to mention vertigo. "Well…nothing else has been easy, so let's give it a try while we have the light." Rock climbing was not a sport on her list of things to experience, but she couldn't give up now.

"We have all day," Matt said, sarcastically. "On the other hand, maybe we'll be out in time for breakfast. You first, Madam." He bowed at the waist.

Matt gave her a boost, and she was able to get a foothold on the first jut. "It's slippery."

"Keep going."

It was with great effort that she grasped ahold of any small crevice available and pulled herself up to the next foothold. Her knee was not kind, as the pain was so sharp that she cried out with every boost of her body.

"I'm right behind you," Matt said, and from the sound of it, having as much difficulty as she with his own injuries.

"I have to rest." Patti said breathlessly. "Oh, God," she said, looking downward. "We're only about 15 feet and I'm dizzy from the height already." She looked upward to the hole, which seemed a mile away. "Matt, I don't think I can do this, I just don't have the skill or the strength."

"We *can* do it. We *have* to do it. Don't look down again. Just think of that breakfast I'm going to buy you once we're out of here."

"Eggs," She hefted herself to the next level.

"Bacon."

"Toast." Another level.

"Raspberry jam."

"Omelet. Lots of cheese."

Her foot slipped. She gripped even harder to the edge of the rock that secured her, but too late. She fell, landing hard on her feet, then onto her knees, she shrieked as the pain bolted through her damaged kneecap. Tears carved a trail through her dirt covered face as she lie on the cavern floor.

Matt speedily returned to ground level, and ran to her side. "Let's see," he said calmly, thankful for the light from above. He straightened her damaged leg and felt the cap. She shrieked.

He removed his shirt, exposing his heavily muscled chest and biceps damp with sweat. With little effort, he quickly tore the shirt into strips. "We're going to wrap this knee and find you a place to rest."

"I'm sorry, Matt. I guess my leg is weak and the walls are slippery. Rock climbing is not my forté. "

After wrapping her knee, he found a safe place—a crevice too narrow for Snapper's head—and helped secure her body inside. "I'm going to see if I can get up top and get immediate help. You sit tight."

"I wish I *could* sit," she said, as she had to lay prone in the crevice, there being no space to sit upright. "Please don't fall and kill yourself. Please get help!" she begged.

"Just stay calm. He can't get to you here."

She watched with trepidation as Matt climbed, rock by slippery rock. At times he had to stop and rest; and, at times, the slippery rocks got the better of him and he nearly fell. She fought the panic; if he should die from a fall, or lay injured, he would be easy prey for Snapper, and no one would ever find her stuck as she was in the wall. She would die in a crevice in a cavern, or be eaten by a giant God-forsaken beast, a freak of nature. No, she did not want to go this way, but all depended on Matt and the climb.

When he was further up the wall, Snapper's putrid odor filled the crevice. She gagged; the odor on an empty stomach was nearly unbearable. "He's found us!" she yelled.

"Keep calm!" Matt answered, his eyes directed upward.

Knowing how fine-tuned were the beast's olfactory senses, she knew without a doubt that he would discover her hidden away in this space, and dreaded what would ensue. She lay quietly, praying that Matt could reach the top and bring help. From this angle, she could watch his progress. All depended on him.

In the filtered light of day, Snapper was even more terrifying than in darkness. Algae hung in grotesque streamers from his immense carapace. His osteoderms bore the result of the shelling by the swat team, leaving him a distorted and monstrous silhouette as he entered the chamber. His claws glistened, long and sharp. Like Arabic swords, they curved menacingly to pointed ends, deadly weapons ready to impale. But his eyes, his snake-like neck, his powerful beak, his flesh, ridged— the color of river bottom—it all painted the picture of a monster beyond the imagination; the horrifying product of genes gone wild.

He filled the immense cavern as he entered, his head bobbing like a dashboard ornament as he perused the situation. He turned to the narrow crevice, his dark eyes penetrating, calculating and terrifying as he viewed her stuffed into the crevice. He then raised his ugly head to focus on Matt and hastened to him, the easier prey.

"Climb! Hurry!" Patti yelled from her niche. "Go! Hurry!"

Matt wasted no time. He reached for the next jutting rock and hefted himself up to a slightly higher level, but it was not yet high enough. Snapper's claws tapped loudly against the chamber floor as he sped to the base of the wall. Then, with one powerful forefoot after another, he raised his body until he was nearly parallel with the rocky wall, his beak snapping ferociously as he aimed for a leg, a foot, any part of the prey that clung desperately to the rocks.

Patti wriggled to the edge of the crevice for a wider view of the dramatic scene. Her heart pounded, sweat poured like rain. *I have to help him!* It was detrimental that Matt make it to safety!

"Hey!" she yelled. "Snapper!" she screamed at the top of her lungs. "Here! Over here!"

"Stop it!" Matted yelled.

"Snapper!" she yelled, ignoring Matt's order. She had to get Snapper's attention. "Climb!" she yelled.

Matt raised himself another foot, then another, but Snapper was clawing at the wall now, trying to catch hold of any part of his body and narrowly missed hooking a shoe. With horror, Patti watched as Snapper projected his massive form off the floor a foot or so, actually *jumping* to catch Matt!

"Just go!" Patti yelled.

Once safely out of reach, Matt paused to rest. Snapper had now given up the chase and was approaching Patti. She wriggled further back into the crevice, her heart pounding as the monster approached. The light diminished as his immense body neared, blocking out the rays, until all she could see was a dark eye, staring. He hissed loudly in frustration.

"You okay?" Matt yelled.

"Yes!" she replied. "Keep going! He can't get me!"

Snapper moved away after a while, but not far enough. As her view of the chamber widened with his departure, she saw him drop his body to rest upon the cavern floor. *Waiting for me....*

Time dragged on as Matt scaled the wall. When, at last, he reached the top, he was a distance of a few feet to the left of the opening. She prayed he could reach it safely— *somehow.*

Again, she inched closer to the edge so she could watch his progress. *"Don't fall...don't fall!"* she whispered. Her body shook in panic as she witnessed him reach out for a handhold of rock. She held her breath, for surely a fall from that height would kill him. He dangled a moment, his feet searching a foothold. She exhaled when he found one. Again, he reached to the next, and the next, like a child on monkey bars, a breathtaking series of moves. Finally, his hands gripped the edge of the opening.

When he was near enough, he attempted to raise himself up and through the hole to daylight, gripping and clawing his way, the balls of his feet searched for any jut of a rock to use as traction. At last, after several failed tries, one God-sent ridge and a final push sent him out of the chamber, his entire body lifted from the cave, and he was out of sight.

He made it! She cried tears of relief, for now, surely, help would be on the way!

CHAPTER TWENTY-EIGHT

There was no way of telling how long Matt had been gone. She lay prone, keeping an eye on Snapper, who was keeping an eye on her. Sometimes he closed his eyes, but with any little sound from her, or from the world above, his eyes shot open, his head raised, and the Arabic curved claws jerked slightly as if ready to spring into action at any given moment.

"Patti!"

She must have dozed off, for the sound of her name woke her from a dream—a nightmare in which she was pursued by an ugly beast. She focused on Snapper who lay like a puppy dog waiting for dinner. *It wasn't a dream.* She wished she could stand and stretch.

"Patti, are you alright?"

At the sound of Matt's voice, Snapper raised his head, looking upward toward the hole in the ceiling.

"Matt? Matt! Thank God you're back!"

"I can see Snapper," he yelled. We have to divert him somehow so we can drop a line to you. We have a winch and harness set up on a truck and we're going to pull you out of there."

"Great!" It was all fine and good, but she was wondering how she could slip out of the crevice without help, considering her damaged knee cap, *and* be hoisted to safety without becoming another meal for Snapper.

"We've just sent a team with recorded voices." he yelled. "They're in the cavern now. Once the paramedics have found Abbot, they'll turn the device on and leave it by the river in the Great Way. If Snapper is attracted to the voices, it should divert him long enough to get you out of there. Tell us when you hear it."

Snapper hissed at the sound of Matt's voice. He raised himself from the floor, the stench of his body permeating the narrow crevice where she lay. He appeared to her as a surreal parade float, decorated in streamers of gray, brown and green matter, a participant in a parade of freakish monsters.

Time passed, leaving Patti to endure Snapper eyeing her—his prey—stuffed into the narrow crevice. When the recorded voices at last drifted into the chamber he turned toward the entrance and listened.

"I hear it!" Patti yelled. "He hears it, too!"

At the sound of her voice, Snapper hissed, and pressed his ugly head against the cavern wall and peered inside the crevice.

"I know you're waiting for me, you bastard," she said to his dark eyeball. He blinked and turned to leave, lumbering through the chamber entrance, and was gone.

"Send the line, hurry!" she yelled, hoping Snapper would not return at the sound of her voice. When it appeared he truly was gone, and with much effort and many abrasions from the sharp rocky edges of the crevice, she slid free, careful to land on her better leg of the two.

The line dropped in slow motion—or so it seemed—as she stood impatiently, one eye glued to the entrance for the return of the beast. *Hurry...hurry...*the line could not drop fast enough! When within reach, she grabbed the basket

"Clip the harness on!" Matt yelled.

She did, and informed him she was ready. The winch began to tighten, and then her feet were off the floor. So focused was she on the rescue, that she was shocked when Snapper returned so quickly.

"Matt!" she screamed. "He's back—hurry!"

It all became a blur, as Snapper now stretched his horrid head beyond her own dangling body, and snapped the line in two. She hit his carapace with a painful thud that knocked the wind from her lungs. Edged between two osteoderms, she tried to catch her breath; but was grateful that Snapper had cut the line instead of her dangling body. Snapper began to spin, amazingly fast for such a huge creature. She quickly grabbed onto a jagged osteoderm and held on for dear life as he tried to toss her off. With the vision of poor Buzz impaled by Snapper's foot fresh in her mind, she was determined not to die in such a horrid manner!

When the beast's menacing head stretched full length to view her on his back, and the killer beak snapped toward her with frightening power and speed, she wriggled backward, drawing her legs to her chest lest he chomp on one. His eyes glared as he snapped and hissed, but so far, she was safe from his reach at this distance. All that mattered was to find a way out of this situation—and quickly! Moving backward on the beast, she thought perhaps she could slide off and run for it. But how, with a hurt knee, and where?

Snapper now changed his approach. He ran toward a rocky wall, ramming himself against it in an attempt to shake her off. When that move failed, he did it again, then again. She screamed, as it was difficult to hang on, even gripping the broken osteoderms which cut into her hands like shards of glass.

One more bump against the wall and she tumbled onto Snapper's massive tail, its boney spikes stabbing at her behind as she bounced downward toward the tip. Then, she was on the ground, and ignoring the pain that shot through her leg and up her spine, she hobbled toward the chamber entrance. It was too late. Snapper was behind her, and she was pinned against a wall.

His height was incredible. He loomed far above her head, but opportunity arose! She eyed the space between the cavern floor and his plastron[iii], and dropped to the floor—careful to not jam her knee on the limestone floor—and dragged her body beneath his, toward his tail. He shifted, realizing she had disappeared. His claws lifted and fell as he turned, and firsthand she witnessed the power in the deadly daggers as they scraped and clicked sharply against the floor. She prayed she would not become impaled on one. Dragging her bad leg, she moved with him; but he was too fast and too smart. Realizing that his prey was beneath him, he sidestepped to expose her ragged body. She rose painfully to her feet, realizing the truth; escape was impossible! She was trapped, and this was the end.

Patti prayed for a quick death as she pressed her quivering body against the cavern wall. Snapper's horrible breath bathed her in stink, and though her eyes were squeezed tightly shut, she felt his presence— smelled his presence— only inches away from tearing her to pieces.

She steadied herself for this horrible end, but then…the ground shook. Then, it shook again… and again….

She peered through narrow slits of eyes, which she had closed in sheer terror, to view Snapper, his neck stretched upward, a periscope perusing the perimeters for impending danger. The sight of him encouraged her for one more attempt to save her life—to bolt and head for the chamber entrance—but within a microsecond of this thought, sections of the floor began to sink. She felt a dip, slight at first, and then, like an hourglass, the flooring sifted within itself. She glanced at Snapper and thought perhaps he had laid down to rest, for his legs had disappeared. It was a confusing moment in which nothing made sense; *Snapper wouldn't stop and rest, and the ground should not shake and sink beneath—sink! We're sinking!*

She screamed as she had never screamed before; earth shattering, like the floor that was caving in beneath her. The thought crossed her mind that perhaps this was a better death than being torn to pieces by a giant freak of nature.

"Matt!" she screamed, having no clue whatsoever if he could even hear her call.

"Ma….!" And she was gone, dirt, rocks, debris pounding her body as she slipped into the abyss.

* * *

"Something else is happening down there. Bring up the line; I'm going down," Matt said. He had witnessed Snapper cut the line and Patti fall onto the beast's back, but everything happened so quickly that he had no clue as to Patti's fate. He heard the blood-curdling scream and a thunderous sound afterward, but that was all. A tremendous plume of dust had risen like an atomic blast forcing him to move away from the hole. When the dust settled, he could see nothing but what appeared to be a dark pit. His eyes were playing tricks, perhaps, because it appeared that the floor of the cavern had disappeared, and Patti with it!

"Hurry up!" he yelled to the winch operator above.

"Gotta get another line and harness!" came the reply.

Matt watched helplessly as the severed line passed his line of vision on its ascent to the top. "How long is this gonna take?" he yelled.

"I've put a call in," came the answer.

* * *

Earlier, shock was the look on the faces of the rescue crews when Matt had appeared out of nowhere back at Buzz's cabin. Once out of the chamber, it had taken a while to orientate himself to the bright daylight, but once he did, he used the sun to calculate in which direction the cabin lay.

Matt came forward through the pine and brush, shirtless, his upper body bleeding from countless abrasions, as well as pants shredded from the sharp edges of rock and limestone. From head to toe, he carried a layer of dark dirt that mingled with the blood of his wounds.

Chet, the reporter, snapped countless photos of his approach and barraged him with questions, of which he answered none, but brushed past the man in silence.

"Good lord!" Sheriff Dave said. "What the hell?"

"What the hell, is right!" Matt yelled. "Where have you all been? We're dying down there. Buzz is dead, Mr. Abbot is nearly dead and Patti is in grave danger, stuck down there with a killer beast. *Nobody* has come to the rescue except for the swat team, and now they're all dead. Well, we need help and right *now!*"

Every uniformed officer jumped to action. The reporter approached, again asking a barrage of questions, and began taking more photos, but Matt pushed him aside. "Get out of here," he yelled. "This is an emergency!"

After he had explained Patti's dire situation, a truck with a winch was located. Now, on the cavern floor, at the edge of the sinkhole above the abyss, and with Patti's first rescue attempt failed, Matt harnessed himself in from the new synthetic line.

"Get another truck, line and harness. Get on it!" he ordered, and then signaled to be lowered into the black hole.

* * *

Patti's head pounded. Something was wrong, but she couldn't remember what, exactly. Her hand reached to touch her eyes. *Are they open?* They were, but vision was nil in the darkness. Her back hurt, and she shifted her body to the right...to the left.... She seemed to be trapped between mountains. *Mountains? Where am I?* A ray of light filtered in and she wondered if she were dead and this was the light to guide her to heaven. This is the story she had heard, anyway, about the light to heaven, but never considered it a reality. She was a scientist, after all.

She moaned as she raised herself onto her elbows by grabbing ahold of one of the mountains. It cut her hand. *How can I grab a mountain?*

Then, it hit her. *Snapper! I'm on Snapper!*

When her eyes adjusted to a minimal light from above, she was able to discern the outline of the beast upon which she sat, but much of him seemed to be covered in dirt and debris. *We fell—we fell through the hole....*

She tried to call for Matt, but her throat was full of dust and dry as a bone. Even as she worked up spit and tried again, it was futile, as she could only project a weak squeal. *He knows where I am. He'll find me. Sit tight.*

* * *

Matt perused the chamber from which he had climbed. That he had scaled its massive, steep walls and survived was nothing short of a miracle, and he blessed whatever stroke of luck, guardian angel, or God, had delivered him safely.

Once lowered, and once he gained footing on the broken floor below, he was aghast at the size and depth of the sinkhole, which was at least twenty feet in width at its widest point. He prayed Patti was still alive. Through it all, she had been a fighter, brave as any soldier in battle, and to be cut short when so close to rescue was unthinkable! He would bring her back—*alive*.

Careful to not sink in himself, Matt lay on his stomach and aimed his headlamp into the pit, which seemed endless as the beam of light faded into its depths.

"Patti!" he yelled. "Can you hear me, Patti?"

After several minutes with no reply, he called into the mic for more line; he would enter the pit himself.

"Not until we send someone else down!" came the reply from above, and Matt waited impatiently while another man was lowered into the chamber. Apparently, the second truck and winch had arrived on the scene.

"Karl," the man said, once standing, and reaching out his hand in greeting.

"Listen, Karl," Matt replied, ignoring the outstretched hand. "Patti Tripp is down there and I'm going to find her. We can't waste another moment; I'm going down. You keep an eye on me."

"Will do," Karl replied.

The dust of the pit filtered through his nostrils, causing him to cough for the first few feet of the descent, after which he made a mental count of the depth of the pit. *10...15....* He wondered how many more feet would slide by before he reached bottom...*20*. He was beginning to lose any shred of hope that Patti was still alive.

* * *

Patti assumed Snapper was dead, as he hadn't moved since she had regained consciousness. *What a way to go, in a dark pit on top of a giant turtle.* It was almost comical, but she couldn't find it in herself to laugh; if Matt didn't come, she would die here.

Then...she cocked her head and listened... had she heard someone? She look upward again, and the stream of light she had seen before seemed to be a bit brighter.

"Matt?" her voice was gravelly. She tried again. "Matt?" When she attempted to scream his name, she gagged on dust at the inhale. Fatigue overcame her, and her entire body throbbed with pain. No longer was it just the knee and legs, it was *everywhere!* She leaned her head against a craggy osteoderms, too exhausted to cry; she would wait.

* * *

"Patti!" Something reflected off his light. He was sure there was an object below, but couldn't quite make it out. Then, her form came into focus leaning between mounds of...*of what? Dirt?*

"Patti, answer me! I can see you!" Whether she was alive or dead, he could not discern, but there she was! "Karl—I see her! Report to top," he yelled

"10-4!" Karl returned. "What will you need down there?"

"A basket. Hurry!"

"Is she breathing?"

"Don't know yet."

* * *

She woke abruptly, thinking she had heard her name called. The light she had seen earlier was very bright and much welcomed, though excessively bright for someone who had been trapped in darkness for such an extended period of time. She shaded her eyes with a filthy hand and blinked against its brilliance.

"I'm here Patti! We'll get you out this time!"

"Matt!" She couldn't contain the relief in her voice. She ached for human contact and reached out to Matt, but he was still several feet above her body. "Get me out," she said weakly. "I've had enough of this silly game."

"Won't be long. Just hang in there." he replied.

For a moment she thought she was imagining things, perhaps shaking from pain—or relief—when her body shifted. The sensation intensified and within seconds she bounced painfully against Snapper's carapace as dirt and debris crumbled and slid from his back. She held tight to the ridged and ragged mound of osteoderm. "He's alive!" she yelled in her hoarse and scratchy voice.

Judging from what little she had noticed of their surroundings, and in the stingy light of Matt's headlamp, which had at least lit the area enough to see outlines of the creature, there was not much room to hide once off of his back, and she was determined to not be in that position; she *had* to stay on, as she had worked too hard to survive and would not lose the battle for her life at this point.

Snapper's long snake-like neck broke through its cover of rock and dirt. As hideous as he had been before, he was twice-fold now. As he craned his neck and turned to view his surroundings, she saw that one eye was missing, leaving mangled strings of bloody flesh in its place. *He can't see me...* and for that she was relieved. Now that she was fully alerted to the situation, she realized that she was sitting on a deep crack in Snapper's carapace. It ran from his tail, diagonally across to the left of his neck. It appeared to her that he was severely injured; but judging by his vicious spirit, he was very much alive, and she was in danger.

"He's alive, Matt! Don't come any further!"

Snapper heard her voice. He twisted his neck in the opposite direction so that his good eye focused on the creature on his backside. She was sure he saw her clearly, as the headlamp highlighted her from above. "Get the beam off me!" she yelled to Matt, and stood, grabbing onto the jagged top of an osteoderm for balance.

Snapper raised full height and turned with his beak snapping dangerously close. His rancid breath now a reminder of the hours and hours of terror she had endured. The fight for life had begun. There were no crevices, no other chambers in which to run. There were no tunnels of escape, just she and Snapper joined in a struggle like no other.

"I'm coming down," Matt yelled, "Be ready!"

Snapper focused his good eye on the light. He turned his body until he was able to stretch his neck upward, hissing and snapping frighteningly close. Matt swung like a pendulum, trying to avoid the deadly jaws.

"Watch out!" Patti yelled, as the beast made a choppy leap just high enough off the ground to send her flying. She landed stomach down on his spikey tail. The adrenaline rush was enough to pull herself up the tail to the broken carapace. She grabbed blindly at the shell until her hand took hold, but only briefly, as a damaged piece of carapace broke off in her grip, forcing her backward. Now she was on the rocky ground, far off of her safety zone. In one brief moment, she had the presence of mind to stick the chunk of carapace into her panties before rising and dragging her injured leg up Snapper's tail to the safety of his backside. Gone was any sensation of pain, as this was a dire and deadly situation, and her only goal was to survive.

Again, she reached for the crack in the shell, and hand over hand she pulled herself from the tail up onto his back. But it was now *she* who was Snapper's target, as he twisted to strike repeatedly—and blindly—as only his empty eye socket was in view. This she witnessed through the sporadic beams of Matt's headlamp as he swung above kicking off from sidewall to sidewall. With no weapon, she was defenseless and could only sit between the osteoderms and pray as Snapper fought against her presence with incredible fury.

"Get ready!" Matt yelled.

She watched the rope lower into the danger zone.

"Get ready to winch fast!" he yelled to Karl, above, who passed the message up top.

She realized what was coming next: it was grab and go. To prepare, she stood, holding onto the osteoderms for balance. She had to keep his attention directed at her, and not at Matt, as he lowered into range of the snapping jaws of death. She called to the beast, thumped his shell with her better leg, and banged on a broken osteoderm. It worked. Snapper hissed, focusing entirely on her and thus blinding himself to Matt's approach.

"Hang onto my legs!" Matt called, now within range.

She reached for them, and missed.

"Come on!" Matt said, and again she tried, but Snapper twisted his neck and now he could see Matt swinging above. His beak opened wide, exposing the dark tunnel of throat in which so many lives had ended.

Matt swung his legs, building momentum until he flew like a man on a trapeze, back and forth, again kicking off from wall to wall, the line creaking with every swing. Snapper's head moved in rhythm to the line, following with his one good eye, perhaps confused at this vision or, perhaps, waiting to strike.

Patti was at a loss of what to do; she certainly couldn't take hold of Matt's legs now! Surely she would miss, fall to the ground, and be impaled by Snapper!

"Jump!" Matt yelled, his breath strained from exertion.

"I can't!" she yelled in return.

"You have to!" he replied, sailing past.

Concentrate...concentrate... her heart pounded in her ears as she waited for the right moment. It would be much easier to put a brake on those legs and climb on, but there was no time for ease, she had to jump, and make it perfect. Time was of the essence, and she could not wait much longer for that perfect opportunity, or for a knee in good working order. "One...two..." she counted. On the count of "three" she leaped off the beast, screaming for the pain in her knee, and striking Matt hard enough to send him swinging and spinning haphazardly around the sinkhole. The beast's jaws snapped like a metronome at this new opportunity, but his missing one eye was in their favor.

"I did it! She thought, clinging to Matt's legs as they swung erratically over the snapping jaws below.

Snapper stretched his neck to break their swing, but Matt managed to push off the beast's head avoiding disaster this time. "Winch!" he yelled, his head bent upward toward the chamber above. "Winch, dammit!"

Blessedly, the line lifted them a foot, then another, and another until they were out of danger.

"I did it!" Patti exclaimed, practically inaudible due to her face being pressed against Matt's legs. It was not an easy task for a woman, who lacked the upper body strength of a man, to hold her own weight in such a way. She was not a true athlete, at least not one who would spend hours at the gym building muscle; but adrenaline raced through her body, giving her a strength born of fear.

As the winch pulled them higher and higher into safety, her fear of having her dangling legs severed by Snapper's mighty beak diminished. Only when they reached the top, would she feel finally free of the beast.

'

CHAPTER TWENTY-NINE

She focused on a single form, black against a bright background. "Where am I?" she whispered, as that was all her voice would allow—a little whisper.

"In a hospital, and safe."

The voice was familiar. She blinked against the bright light and opened her eyes wide. Slowly, she focused the shock of black hair, the black-rimmed glasses, the slight Asian figure.... "Kim?"

"It's me," he replied. "In the flesh—*living flesh*, I might add."

"Liv...?" Then, it dawned on her. She reached out a weak hand, which he took into his own. "You're alive...I'm so glad," she said, weakly.

"Me, too. When you're better, I'll tell you all about it."

"Am I okay?"

"Yep. Can't keep a good scientist down. You have a badly bruised patella, but it's not broken. Lots of abrasions and stitches here and there. You're a bit of a mess, but alive!"

"What happened with Mr. Abbot?"

"He's still in the hospital, but he's a sturdy old devil. He'll be going to a nursing home."

"I'm glad he's okay."

* * *

A few days later, she was sitting up in the hospital bed with Kim beside her in a chair.

"I've never been so terrified in my life," Kim said, his eyes wide, reliving the horrible event. "It was a lucky break that we had reached an area in the river where there was a foot of airspace, because when that monster took Steve, the oxygen went with him. I was stranded. I had no idea how far back you were, and was afraid to call out for fear of Snapper returning. I prayed that he was really gone, but sad for Steve. After all, he died saving my life." He shook his head settling his eyes on his lap.

"It's not your fault, Kim."

"I know, but I wish I could forget."

"Me too. But go on, I need to hear the rest."

"I paddled—with one arm— and kicked my feet to get to the wall and held onto rocks or whatever I could find. After a while it dawned on me that Snapper would return, and I'd be waiting like a sitting duck; so I took the chance and swam—if you could call it that." Sometimes I had to float because none of this was easy with my arm the way it was, and it hurt like hell." He was quiet a moment. "It took forever to reach the gate at the entrance, and when I did, I cried like a baby. I prayed that you were okay, Patti."

"I know you did."

"My arm was throbbing like the devil, but I managed to climb out of the river and walk. I walked and walked like in a trance, not knowing which way to go. It was like my memory had been removed. All I knew was that there was a horrible beast down below, and I had to get away."

"I know that feeling."

"It started to get dark, and I was still wandering. When I came to a road, I flagged down a truck and got a ride to the hospital. And poor you, stuck down there with that freak."

* * *

Three days later, Patti sat at her kitchen table, coffee cup in hand and one leg stretched out toward the kitchen sink. A black elastic brace secured her healing patella. How long had Snapper ruled her days? At least she was healing quickly now, after days long and dull in the hospital because of *him*.

Kim refilled their coffee cups and sat opposite. "I can't wait for the DNA results. Smart girl, you were, tucking that piece of carapace into your undies."

"I'm as anxious and excited as you are. It's baffling how he got to that size. What if it caused by an outside agent? If so, that possibility needs to be examined immediately. God forbid this happens again. *Or, is it genetic?*"

"Let's hope it's *not* genetic. We have no proof of anything like this ever happening anywhere else in the world."

"Any news on the search?" she asked.

"I'm keeping up on it, but they haven't gone down again. Matt's helping put a search party and plan together. Speaking of Matt, haven't you heard from him?"

"Nope."

"Has he called?"

"Nope."

"I'm shocked. After all you've been through?"

"I kind of thought the same thing, but…who knows? Maybe he wants to forget the entire nightmare, and I can't blame him." She shrugged, but had wondered several times why hadn't come to visit, or at least called. "At least you're keeping me posted."

* * *

The following week, the DNA results were delivered FedEx to Patti's front door. She and Kim sat again at the kitchen table staring at the envelope. "This is it," she said. "The moment of truth."

"Open!" Kim rubbed his hands together. "I can't contain myself any longer. I gotta know the truth."

"Here goes." Patti slit the envelope open with a kitchen knife and removed a letter along with another few pages of DNA genetic codes. Setting the codes aside, she glanced over the letter. "…jeez…," she whispered.

"Well? Come on, share!"

"Aside from formalities, here's the rundown: *Macrochelys suwanniensis, Alligator Turtle.*

"Suwannee River habitat," Kim said. "No surprise, there."

"Right. Now wait…." She read on.

"Oh my God, you won't believe this. Look!"

She set the letter on the table so he could read for himself. "…a mutant gene of extraordinary circumstance. When running the DNA sample through our database we discovered that it matched the DNA of [iv]*Stupendemys geographicus* dating from the Miocene period approximately 23 million years ago. This is an unparalleled discovery, and we have petitioned the DNR of Georgia for permission in uncovering the body of this reptile for future study."

"Wow," Kim said. "Guess we've hit the 'discovery' jackpot."

"Oh, and look at this. We've been calling Snapper a *'he'*. Well *'he'* is a *'she'*! Guess I was too busy trying to survive to notice."

"Hopefully, *she* didn't have a boyfriend out there."

Patti stared blankly at Kim.

"What? I'm joking."

"Maybe not."

"What do you mean?"

"Judging from the information Buzz gave us regarding Snapper being his father's pet way back in the '30's, I'd say she is around eighty years old, and they can normally live to one-hundred. I think it takes about twenty years to reach around fifty pounds—and I repeat—in a *normal* snapper. How big was she at age twenty? Maybe she was normal size; and if so, she was living a normal life, and that means *mating*. She could have laid hundreds or even thousands of eggs before she evolved into a monster. And, male sperm can remain active up to three years before she allows it to fertilize."

"Snapper 101. If she laid eggs 60 years ago, they either hatched, or never matured."

"What if…?"

"Stop! I don't want to hear about it!" Kim replied, covering his ears.

Patti shot him a disgusted glance. "What if…" she continued. "What if she *did* lay eggs? She can fertilize them herself when she's ready, providing she's encountered a male at some point in time."

"But that doesn't make sense." Kim said. "Normally there's a time span for fertilization. Hers should be ancient history by this time."

"But there is nothing *normal* about this, Kim. Suppose she's laid eggs over the past sixty years. If they've remained dormant and unfertilized, can she still fertilize them? A young turtle takes a while to grow, and if there's a mutant, who knows? Maybe out of hundreds of eggs there will be one mutant, like Snapper."

Kim laid his forehead on the table. "What is it you want to do, Patti? What treacherous plan are you leading to?"

"Let's look again at the data you collected on missing people along the rivers. Then let's call Matt."

CHAPTER THIRTY

O nce Chet, the reporter, spread the news of a gargantuan, beastly alligator turtle trapped in a cavern beneath a small town in Georgia, Snapper became national news. A siege of broadcasters from around the world spilled into Riverside. The three hotels in the area could not handle the hordes of people, and therefore, the town was surrounded by tent cities, or parking lots of the rented RV's of media mongers and curious onlookers. The local police were inundated with either prank or serious calls from folks who swore a beast such as Snapper had crossed their paths, or had appeared in their yards.

"This is a nightmare!" said Sheriff Dave. "We're busting at the seams. We've had to deputize citizens just to help keep the crowds away from the river! And the prank calls...the phones haven't stopped ringing. Let's get that damn beast out of there and get back to normal."

"That's what we're doing, Sheriff, "Matt replied. They stood alongside Patti, Kim, Karl, town officials and scientists, statewide and foreign, watching as two cranes were set in place aside the cavern opening from which Matt had safely rescued Pattie. Karl, who had helped in the rescue several weeks earlier, was again paired with Matt to secure chains around the beast in order to lift her from the pit. There was no doubt she was dead, considering the injuries she sustained in the fall.

A semi truck with an open flatbed trailer attached, waited for its heavy cargo. Patti and Matt wondered if the beast would even fit on the flatbed, and what a commotion it would bring while being escorted to a waiting barge in Savannah. An entourage of motorcycle police were at the ready to guide the truck down the highway.

Harnessed and secured by the cranes, Matt and Karl descended first into the chamber, and then into the sinkhole. All the while, the men searched for Snapper's body by shining their headlamps into the pit. "I don't see her, do you?" Matt asked Karl, still several feet above him.

"Not yet," came the reply. "She should be visible at any moment."

Matt thought it unusual that the putrid scent of the decaying beast had not yet reached their nostrils. When they touched ground, they stared incredulously at the empty pit.

"You won't believe this," Matt said into the mic attached to his helmet.

"What's happening?" came the response from above.

"She's gone!"

Silence. "How's that possible?"

Matt settled his lamp on a large opening in the wall of the sinkhole.

"It looks like she's still alive after all. There's a large hole in a sidewall, and she's dug herself out. Pull us up. We're not prepared to deal with a gargantuan, injured alligator turtle. Looks like we need weapons"

* * *

Patti questioned Matt relentlessly over coffee afterward: was there blood? Were there tracks, and how thick was the wall through which she escaped? Considering Snapper's mortal injuries, she should have been dead. Her disappearance was major news. Everyone was baffled. Police station phones rang off the walls as panic spread.

"I'm going with you," Patti said, after hearing that Matt planned on returning to the sinkhole for a search and destroy mission.

"You're not."

"I'm a scientist."

"I don't care; you barely made it out alive the last time, not to mention you're now sporting a brace around your knee."

"I'm like new, look...." she stretched her leg outside the booth and lifted it up and down, not mentioning the shock of pain that shot straight up to her hip joint. "And, speaking of which, why didn't you visit me at the hospital?"

"I did, you just don't remember."

"I owe you my life. You could have come while I was coherent."

"You needed to recover. I figured you needed time, time to mourn Ted, time to heal. The last thing you needed was to be reminded of our harrowing misadventure.

"We're practically a team now," she said. I'm going back with you. We'll follow the new passage, and we'll find her. We're the only ones living who have had the experience of dealing with such a creature. I can't imagine how she survived with the injury across her carapace, but she was apparently strong enough to dig herself out of that mess."

"Where could she go? What's down there? Another chamber? Another exit into the river?"

"We're going to find out."

"You're one brave—and foolish— scientist."

"I have to redeem myself. I was a coward down there."

"You were far from cowardly."

* * *

Instead of air tanks, Matt carried a flame thrower as he was lowered into the sinkhole. Patti followed, with camera ready; she needed footage of the beast. Karl was also lowered into the pit. Strapped to his back he carried an automatic assault rifle. They fully expected that the prehistoric beast had died of her wounds. Their job was to seek and destroy (if necessary). Her body was to be exhumed from the cavern for study.

Once mustered on the floor of the pit, headlamps lit, weapons ready, they entered through the passage that Snapper had carved with her claws. The injured beast did not have to claw far, for after only a few short feet, the passage entered into a huge chamber.

"I wonder if this is another entrance into the Great Way?" Patti asked.

"It doesn't look familiar," Matt replied, spinning a 360 with his headlamp.

"There's a very earthy smell, like dirt. Odd. You wouldn't think there would be dirt beneath the upper chambers."

"It's very damp, too," Karl said, as they walked forward, ever cautious that as far stretched as it seemed, Snapper could appear at any moment.

"Hmm. Not a bad place for a nest." Patti said.

"I'd hate to think of that possibility."

A fork in the passage came into view, and the trio stopped.

"We'd best stick together," Matt said.

"I say left."

"I can't see much difference, Karl."

"Then it doesn't matter. That should resolve the question." Patti started forward on the left fork, and the rest followed. After a time, she leaned over and grabbed a handful of dirt. "This really is odd. In the chambers above, the floor is all limestone rock. Here, it's mostly dirt. Somewhere, this opens out onto land."

But it didn't open out onto land, at least not in the distance they traveled. When they came to another fork, they turned back.

"We don't want to get lost down here." Matt said. "Let's go back and try the other fork."

The three headlamps brightened their passage like daylight as they continued the investigation into the other fork. Aside from the stone walls and dirt floor, there was nothing unusual until Patti stopped in her tracks.

"Smell that?" she asked in a whisper.

"Sure do," Karl answered, readying his automatic weapon.

Matt did the same, securing the flame gun in his hands and aiming straight ahead.

Patti switched on the camera, trying in vain to shake off a spasm of fear that shook her body. She strained to steady the shaking of her hands; she need a steady hold on the camera for the necessary photos.

They continued forward without sight of the beast. Ahead, the passage curved to the left, and not knowing what was around the bend, they stopped, pressing themselves against the left wall of the tunnel. Matt peeked around the curve, his light illuminating nothing but a long passage that wound to the right. They traveled forward, quietly stepping over the uneven floor and once more pressed against the right side tunnel wall at the curve. The stench of Snapper was overpowering, even more so than they had ever experienced beforehand.

"She must be dead; it reeks," Karl said nearly inaudibly.

As soon as Matt's headlamp lit the passageway around the bend, a tremendous uproar sent them stumbling backward.

"My God!" Matt yelled. "Retreat!"

Patti did not stop to view the source of the commotion. She turned and ran back through the tunnel, her headlamp illuminating splotches of wall and floor as she pumped her legs, unmindful of her healing knee. After some distance, she turned to see if Matt and Karl were following, but the passage was empty. The sound of gunfire shattered her eardrums. The flame thrower went into action, lighting the tunnel in an alarming, sudden flash; but she could view none of the action. The terrifying thought crossed her mind that she could be the last one standing on this day, and she did not know if she could reach the sinkhole in time to be lifted to safety. "Matt!" she yelled. "Karl!"

No answer. She was torn between returning to find them, or continue to the waiting harnesses. Her weight shifted from one leg to the other, ready to fly in either direction, but at that moment of indecision, Matt rounded the bend. "Go!" he yelled.

"Where's Karl?"

"Behind me!"

In the millisecond before turning away, she spotted Karl running like the wind. "Move!" he yelled. "They're coming!"

They? Patti took off like a scared deer. *They? Are there more?*

Almost to the sinkhole, and the lines and harnesses that would carry them to safety, she heard a horrific scream. Her chest hurt; she could barely breathe from the exertion. Her heart beat like a jackhammer, but it didn't stop her from bringing the camera to her eye. Matt scrambled toward her, the flame thrower gun gripped in his hands and bouncing haphazardly with each stride. *Click.* He was safe, but Karl had fallen victim to a voracious pair of car-sized alligator snappers, their bodies grotesque and horrific in the flash of the headlamps. *Click.* Karl screamed as their powerful beaks repeatedly and viciously dug into his flesh. Patti ran closer to the gruesome scene. *Click.* In the flash of the camera, she cringed at the sight of Karl in a futile attempt to fight off the vicious creatures.

Matt, with flame thrower in hand, backtracked to within several feet of Karl's flailing body.

"Save him!" Patti screamed, but stood as helpless as him, for if he used the flame thrower, he would incinerate Karl! Matt ran at the beasts, frantically banging on one spiked carapace.

Click. Patti trembled like leaves in a windstorm as she recorded this surreal nightmare.

"Get off!" Matt yelled, kicking and pounding at the creature at hand, but the hideous, aggressive beasts paid him no mind. They were intent on shredding their prey to pieces, and their prey no longer yelled or moved; he was surely dead.

Matt and Patti retreated quickly, without looking back at the bloody carnage, to the harnesses that awaited them. Weary, defeated and shocked, their eyes turned to the waiting harness that would have no passenger on the return.

CHAPTER THIRTY-ONE

"We saw two," Matt reported to the council of scientists, state troopers, local police, and National Guardsmen, who sat listening intently to his words. "I'd say they were the size of a Volkswagen beetle, wouldn't you, Patti?"

The room at the municipal building was filled with folding chairs and plenty of paparazzi.

Patti sat beside Matt at the long table generally reserved for the town council or other official meetings. An emergency meeting had been called immediately upon the rescue of Patti and Matt from the sinkhole. The photos Patti had taken of Karl's horrifying death were labeled "High Priority" and "Confidential", shown only to the scientists, high ranking officials of the National Guard, police, the mayor, and locked in a safe.

Needless to say, tensions ran high and fear was rampant. The elementary and high schools were closed until further notice, and folks in general were sticking close to home. The curious out-of-town on-lookers had been sent away and roadblocks were stationed at all points leading in and out of the town. Police were sent to interview the callers who reported seeing giant turtles in their yards, calls to which the police had paid no heed prior to the new discovery of more beasts.

Patti stood. "The one thing we're certain of is that these creatures are extremely dangerous. They have voracious appetites. They hunt; they kill. I'm guessing that the turtles that killed Karl are approximately twenty to thirty years old, but it's hard to say. Snapper is a freak of nature, and in layman's language, she carries the mutant gene of a giant turtle that lived 23 million years ago. She's a dinosaur. When Elmer Abbot found the turtle back in the 1930's, she was of normal size. He kept her as a pet until she escaped in 1966.

Why is this happening now? My fellow colleague and marine biologist, Kim Su, and I, have gone over the reports of people—cold cases—missing up and down this river and its tributaries over the last decades, and our deductions are that many of this missing cold cases could very well be the result of Snapper and her offspring. It *has been* happening all along, but we didn't see it. This is why Ted Lane was investigating the waters in our river; he was searching for the reason our river is practically void of life.

We don't know how many years Snapper maintained a breeding size, but, as we know, she did mate and produce offspring. In the real world, the female alligator turtle, after mating, can fertilize her eggs from the male sperm up to three years. Because of the complexity of this case, we don't know what the time period would be for Snapper, but apparently longer than three years. Today, we witnessed two turtles of gargantuan size, but don't know if Snapper is still alive, or if there are others."

Patti sat, shaken, remembering Karl's horrid death. She felt guilty for taking a photo of his death scene; but on the other hand, it was necessary. She could justify her action, but it was still hard to swallow.

The meeting continued. Strategies were discussed in ways of annihilating the creatures that lived beneath their town. First, though, they needed more information on the number of turtles that lived below and began to configure a search team. Patti could feel the tension in Matt's body, so close to hers at the table, and knew he was distressed that he had not yet been named in the search team.

"Include me," he said, standing to address the committee. I'm familiar with the beasts, and I've been through the chambers; I know what to expect."

"And me," Patti said, rising to stand next to him.

"Sit down," Matt said quietly and tapped her on the leg.

"No way. We're a team," she whispered in return.

* * *

The following day, the team was ready: Matt, Patti, and eight National Guardsmen. Between them, they held a menagerie of weaponry, including flame throwers, assault rifles, and one high powered tranquilizer gun. The visiting scientists (and herself) insisted on capturing one of the beasts for scientific study. The theory was that the creature would be deeply tranquilized and kept in that state perpetually until it had been safely lifted from the cavern, then airlifted to the science lab in Charleston, penned and examined. The science lab in Charleston was, with Kim barking orders, scrambling to build a temporary compound that could contain a beast of that size while they built a permanent enclosure. Required were water, land, no shortage of food and very high, strong walls. Patti hoped this plan did not go asunder.

* * *

After a quick refresher on using an assault rifle—the one flung over her shoulder— Patti and the group were lowered into the cave to begin the search, radios, mics and headlamps, on. With a camera strapped around her neck, she was armed and ready to shoot in either definition of the term, camera, or ammo.

Matt lead the way, followed by the eight National Guardsmen, and then, reluctantly last, Patti. She wondered how she could photograph whatever they discovered ahead from the back row, but then worried about Matt, first in line. His courage was amazing, and she was determined to match it with her own. The beams from the headlamps bounced dramatically from wall to wall as the group tread carefully ahead, constantly scanning the area.

"Halt," Matt whispered, and the group stopped.

Patti craned her neck to get a glimpse of him and then squeezed her way through the men to stand with the front line. The guardsman to her right gave her a penetrating look of annoyance, one that she didn't particularly like, so she eyed him back, shining her headlamp directly into his eyes until he turned to look ahead.

The group had halted at the last curve before the creatures had appeared the day before. Matt peered around the bend, and then motioned the group to move forward, but silently.

The reek of a decaying animal filled their nostrils. The men, much to their credit, did not show any reaction to the putrid odor, but proceeded silently, following Matt into the unknown territory. She removed herself to the back of the group, suspecting at any moment for all hell to break loose. The fact that it didn't, was even more frightening, adding to the tension of the moment. *Where are the beasts?* Not knowing, sent shivers up her spine!

Matt had stopped again, and now the silence was broken. "Whew, will you look at that thing!" one of the men remarked, and Patti walked forward until she stood next to Matt in the lead. They had entered a larger chamber; and there, highlighted ahead in the ten beams of light from the headlamps, lay Snapper's immense corpse, putrid, decaying, *and not intact.* The spikey tail Patti had once landed upon in the sink hole was nearly chewed to the carapace. One mighty razor-sharp claw, now severed and still, lay dormant next to a half-eaten foreleg. Of the great head, most was chewed through, the large piercing beak hanging by bits of flesh. The severe crack in the carapace had now weakened with decay and was in the process of splitting in half. The smell was sickening.

"My God. They've been eating her!" Patti said, unable to take her eyes away.

The group moved forward in unison, headlights bouncing off walls, crevices and dark corners searching for any hint of danger, any sign of the two beasts that had killed Karl. As they reached the putrid corpse, much mumblings and exclamations over the beast's size and odor echoed throughout the chamber until Matt told them to hush.

"We don't know where those creatures are, so keep your voices down. We're sitting ducks here. Spread out and search for the other two."

The men searched the area while Patti snapped dozens of photos. Gagging, and holding back the bile that threatened to erupt from her gut, she took dozens of photos from every angle, after which she, too, began to investigate the cavern for any signs of broken or whole eggs that could have been deposited in this place.

"Hey, Patti."

She turned to see Matt a short distance away, waving her toward him.

"Look." He shined his lamp toward the body of water flowing to the right. "I'm thinking this way leads to the Great Way."

"Look how wide and deep it is here. We have to find out where this river comes from." She shined her light to the left as far as the beam would allow a clear vision of its flow and curve. "We've got to get up there, Matt. We have no idea where this originates from. The water is deep enough for the turtles that killed Karl. "

"First, we need to let them know above that we've found Snapper. In her condition I think it's best she remai...."

Shots rang out. Weapons fired, and the cavern lit in a blast of light from a flare gun. Matt spun around searching for the direction of action. Men's voices cried out in alarm; and from the passage from which they had entered, came a beast—hissing, jaws snapping—a hideous and deadly creature whose only intent was to kill.

The beast's head swung from side to side, its eyes searching for the intruders. The lucky ones found crevices in which to squeeze, while two guardsmen slipped behind Snapper's putrid corpse. The others ran helter-skelter, looking for cover.

As the beast moved further into the cavern, another came from the river behind Patti and Matt.

"Look out behind you!" a guardsman yelled. Matt and Patti glanced behind, shocked to see the grotesque creature climb out of the river. They stood in the balance, one beast coming from behind and another blocking escape from the passage.

"We're trapped!" Patti said. "Tranq gunner!" she screamed. Matt jerked her from her spot by her shirt collar and literally dragged her to a craggy wall a few steps away. "Climb!" he shouted.

"I don't want them to kill both!" she yelled over the explosion of gunfire. Flamethrowers sporadically lit the chamber and was the only light bright enough to catch a glimpse of the chamber in its totality.

"Get moving!" Matt yelled, giving her a boost onto the first foothold.

She continued upward, this climb much easier than the cavern from which she had been rescued. Rocks, spotlighted in her headlamp, jutted out, almost as if nature had provided for this moment on purpose.

"Don't look...don't look..." Patti whispered as she grabbed one protruding rock after another until she reached a rocky ledge. She boosted herself up and turned. "We're high enough, Matt!"

He was close behind, and when both sat overlooking the scene below, they were helpless to assist the men who were now trapped in a horrifying battle of life and death. They were voyeurs in a game of chess, where all pawns were in checkmate.

Patti gripped hard onto Matt's forearm. "I need one of those creatures alive!" she said.

"And I need all those men alive," he answered, shaking her arm off. "What are you thinking? We need to save their lives *first!*"

She shrank back, ashamed. Of course the men should come first!

To the right, to the left, chaos reigned. Flame throwers lit up the cavern in a hot, fiery glow. Weapons fired, adding to the concert of hell, sparks flew from gunfire. The beast that had blocked the passageway, now moved forward. Patti directed her light to his movements. He headed directly across the chamber toward two guardsmen.

"Enough!" Matt said, and swung his body off the ledge.

"Stay here!" Patti yelled, her light fixed onto the top of his head as he descended. He was quickly on the ground, his weapon drawn. He fired his automatic, running the circumference of the chamber and jumping over the stinking remains of Snapper's tail, he disappeared behind the rotting course.

Where's that promised courage now? Patti chastised herself for not taking action and descended her protective ledge without further thought. Once her two feet touched dirt, the atmosphere quickly changed from voyeur to participant; it was chaos! Weapons blasted, flame throwers lit the chamber into a glowing orange world, and death by friendly fire was a true possibility.

The chaos calmed only when the hideous beasts were contained by the threat of the flame throwers now held by Matt and another man. The beasts had the men pinned against a stony wall. Patti skirted the center of the chamber, running the circumference to stand by Matt. From this angle, she saw that one beast had been charred. Half his head was black, one eye totally gone, burned away by flame. Part of his carapace had been incinerated as well, chunks of it gone, leaving a jagged and unnatural black edge. The beasts were obviously terrified of the fire as they stood, hesitant to pounce.

"Shoot the injured one!" Patti yelled. "Don't kill the other! Where's the guy with the tranq gun?"

"Dead. Out there." Matt pointed the flame thrower gun toward the body in the center of the chamber.

Patti eyed the gun laying a short distance from the corpse, and then eyed the two beasts. She would have to pass them by before she could retrieve the gun.

"Don't you dare," Matt warned, as if reading her mind.

"Hold them at bay!" she yelled; and without reply she ran an arc around the beast nearest her, not mindful that the creature had caught her movement in the corner of its eye—it's *one* remaining eye. It turned and followed, gaining speed with every step, and with Matt at its tail.

"Circle around!" He ordered to the guardsmen scattered throughout the chamber.

"No!" she shrieked, when a sudden force threw her to the ground. Surely she was to die in the jaws of a beast!

"Hold your fire!" Matt yelled, and then… "Are you crazy?" Matt now lay over her prone body. She had been tackled!

"The tranq gun!" she said breathlessly, as the weight of his body pressed the air from her lungs. She stretched an arm toward the tranquilizer gun which lay a foot from her grasp. A brief glimpse of the dead guardsman sprawled close by registered a bloody head, a faceless torso, and a mass of brain matter. In the fraction of a second, the vision locked itself in memory, to return again in an obscure and unwelcomed flash of recall.

Matt stretched an arm over hers, grasped the gun and then rolled to a crouching position. The beast was nearly on them. He motioned for Patti to stand. "Stay low!" Again, he grabbed her shirt, and they scrambled like crabs toward the oncoming beast.

"What are you doing?" she screamed, thinking he had lost his mind.

A few inches from a grizzly death, he shoved Patti off to the right, while he dove to the left of the creature barreling forward.

"Fire! Fire!" he yelled. As the beast charged through the empty space between them, its beak snapping like steel doors slamming shut, a cacophony of ear-shattering blasts flew in deafening succession. The creature stumbled and fell, his neck stretched to its length, his head lolling to one side, exposing the charred remains of what was once his face. He was dead.

"Don't kill the other!" Patti screamed as she scrambled to her feet. She had stumbled and rolled when Matt tossed her aside, but now stood, a ragged, dirt covered soul begging to spare the one remaining horrid creature that, having witnessed its partner's death, now came at her.

The familiar and terrifying sound of snapping jaws paralyzed her with fear, yet she stood steady in this theater of the macabre. "Shoot the dart!" she screamed to Matt, having no clue as to where he was now, or *if* he still was. She had lost sight of him. Dirt filled her eyes, and the only vision she saw was the blur of a beast rapidly advancing.

Then, she heard it, the dart gun had fired! The beast stumbled slightly as the dart sank into his neck. He braked, shook his head, eyed his prey, stepped forward and stopped again. Patti remained still, waiting for the drug to take effect.

Matt and the soldiers surrounded the beast, weapons aimed and ready to fire, if necessary. Patti held her breath, stepping backward, waiting for the tranquilizer to work—*praying* that the tranquilizer would work fast. It did. The beast's head began to droop and its body waver. It could not fight the effects of the powerful tranquilizer any longer and settled to the floor, retracting its head and appendages into the safety and protective armor of its carapace.

"I hope I never see another one of those things." The voice of a guardsman broke the dead silence that followed.

"Me too," Patti whispered under her breath as sighs of relief echoed throughout the cavern, but none as well appreciated as her own; she would bring a dinosaur to the science lab. The live one would be delivered, and Patti was sure the transport would be a lot lighter than the truck driver had first anticipated.

CHAPTER THIRTY-TWO

Patti and Matt drove together to Charleston to witness in person, the beast's new home.

"You and the team did some fantastic job," Patti said as she, Matt and Kim stood on the walkway overlooking the compound.

"We tried." Kim replied. "Nothing is too good for Snappie."

"Snappie?"

"Yeah, that's what we call him, and we *think* it's a *him*, by the way. We did a quick examination of the plastron while he was still tranquilized and hoisted on the crane, but we don't have another turtle of his size for comparison. The tail is thick, claws very long, plastron seems to be concave, all signs of a male specimen; but because he's a mutant, we just don't know for sure. If we had another one to......"

"You can forget that!" Patti blurted. "I'm not ready, and besides, the other one is probably a stinking pile of decay by this time."

"You need to come back, Patti. We need you. You're missing out on the biggest discovery since...since...well, just *since*."

"It's an *amazing* discovery, Kim. We're lucky we survived, but....

"But?"

"I'll be working with the DNR now. It's important that we monitor the river and bring it back to life. We don't know if there are more of these mutant creatures out there, but you can be sure that I'll be watching.

"It is a fabulous set up, Kim. I must admit." Matt interjected, much to Patti's relief.

"Thanks, Matt. Coming from you, that's a great compliment."

"How so?" he asked.

"Well…you know… big macho guy saves the day, overpowers giant beast to save the damsel in distress. It just seems like you'd rather see Snappie dead than alive."

"Now, wait a minute…." Matt protested. "I do have a heart, you know."

"Honestly, Kim." Patti cut in, disgusted. "And 'damsel'? You're referring to me as a 'damsel'? Just *who* survived hours in a cave with a giant man-eating turtle? I resent that!"

"Oh, you know what I mean! Of course I don't think you're a 'damsel'. Jeez, sensitive, aren't you?"

"Look, there's…uh…*Snappie,*" Matt said, pointing to the large osteoderms as they broke through the water line in the man-made pond that had been built especially for his needs and size.

All eyes turned to the beast in the pond.

"He knows we're here," Patti said, goosebumps creeping up her arms. "Look how he watches us."

"I do appreciate seeing him from this distance, and not one on one." Matt said. "One day he may be nearly as big as his mother. What will you do then with this open air pen, Kim? You'll have to raise the rails, so to speak."

"It's in the plan, Matt…in the plan."

"They live a long time, you know."

"I'm a scientist. Of course I know."

* * *

"Patti," Matt said, hands on the steering wheel, eyes ahead, as they rolled along the highway on the return to Riverside. "I know this is probably too soon, but do you think you might go out to dinner with me sometime? *Just* dinner. Nothing more."

"Why, Matt…uh, you never did tell me your last name."

"Wojciechowski."

"What?"

"It's Polish."

"Spell it."

"Don't worry about it. So? What do you say to dinner one night?"

She looked at him and smiled. "Tonight's good. We're a team, remember?"

"Great!" Matt replied, smiling. "What do you say to stopping by 'home base' on the way home?"

Patti was silent. She hadn't been at the site by the river that had started the entire series of horrifying events since the memorial plaque was cemented into the ground.

"Okay," she said quietly after much thought.

* * *

"In Memory of those who lost their lives in the most paramount turtle hunt in history."

Patti reached up and ran her finger over Ted's name. Once the jolt of pain passed, she was able to concentrate on the others who had lost their lives to Snapper.

Theodore Lane, DNR, Sheriff Arthur Monroe, Jack Moss, Search and Rescue...and the list continued.

"...all those lives." Matt said, reading over her shoulder. "What a waste. It's a wonderful plaque, but '...*the most paramount turtle hunt in history?*' A little corny, wouldn't you say?"

"What else could we call it, Matt? It *was* the most paramount turtle hunt in history."

Beneath the list of dead were these words:

Please respect our wildlife. They are our National Treasure.

"I like this part." He tapped the last line with his index finger. We don't need a nation of turtle killers. It's bad enough some people go out of their way to crush them in the roads."

"I worry about that, too. Snapper and her brood were freaks of nature."

"We hope."

"We hope," Patti dittoed. "There's no way of knowing whether Snapper deposited eggs elsewhere, or not. At least we're alerted to that possibility, and you can be sure I'll be watching like a hawk for news of people missing mysteriously along the rivers. Even if Snapper did deposit more eggs, there is no way of knowing if any other offspring carry the dinosaur gene unless something happens, or we run DNA samples on every alligator turtle from here to the Mason-Dixon line."

"Speaking of turtles...." Matt said, pointing over her shoulder.

She turned toward the river to see a small turtle climbing onto the bank to bask in the sun. It eyed them suspiciously, and then crawled toward the log which had held Ted's neatly folded clothes on the day he disappeared.

"It's an alligator snapper. Look at the spikes," she said, picking the creature up by its carapace. I wonder...."

The turtle instinctively retracted into its shell.

"Go on, you wonder what?"

"You know, I think we ought to take this one in for a DNA test. It's probably nothing to worry about, but who knows."

As Matt steered the car down the dusty access road, Patti held the turtle up at eye level. "Come on out, buddy. I'm not going to hurt you."

"One day we should finish the search of the river, see where it ends down there in the sinkhole chamber." Matt said.

"Well there you are!" Patti cooed as the turtle extended its neck first, and then it's appendages. It pumped its legs rapidly against the open air, while long, sharp claws sparked tiny bursts of reflected sunlight. All the while its hooded, dark eyes stared steadily into hers.

"You're a handsome fellow, aren't you," she said, returning the turtle's stare.

"You're getting a little too close, aren't you?" Matt said, one eye on Patti and the turtle, the other on the road.

"I don't think his neck can stretch this far yet. What was it you were saying, about the river?" She turned to look at Matt.

"We should get down there one of these days and explore the underground river. What if there are more of those monsters making a home in the cavern? What if that's one right there in your hands, and why do you insist on holding it so close?"

"I'm examin...."

SNAP!

THE END...*or is it?*

ABOUT THE AUTHOR

Jocelyn Miller writes from the beautiful Chesapeake Bay in Maryland, and Pine Island, Florida, where she lives with her husband, Bernard, two Yorkshire Terriers, and an Amazon Parrot.

Other books by Jocelyn Miller

Broken Chords
Tanglewood Plantation
Tanglewood Plantation II, Adventure in the Everglades
Tanglewood Plantation III, Adventure in New Orleans

All books are available at in paperback or kindle at www.amazon.com

---

[i] The Power Head is a slip on, one-time weapon comparable to an A-K 47 round. It can be slipped over the head of a spear gun and fired in order to injure or kill attacking sharks while diving.

[ii] The material in which dive suits are made

[iii]Plastron: the underside of a turtle's shell

[iv] Miocene Period, approximately 23 million years ago

www.ingramcontent.com/pod-product-compliance
Lightning Source LLC
Chambersburg PA
CBHW070007260626
47159CB00005B/1711